Maleficence of Magnolia

A. L. LaFleur

authorHOUSE®

AuthorHouse™
1663 Liberty Drive
Bloomington, IN 47403
www.authorhouse.com
Phone: 1 (800) 839-8640

Published by AuthorHouse   12/14/2015

ISBN: 978-1-5049-6648-1 (sc)
ISBN: 978-1-5049-6647-4 (hc)
ISBN: 978-1-5049-6646-7 (e)

Library of Congress Control Number: 2015920222

Print information available on the last page.

This book is printed on acid-free paper.

Chapter One

Maggie Sumner slowly began to rouse from her luxurious slumber, blinking several times, having difficulty placing her surroundings. The feel of the silken sheets and thick down comforter told her where she was before she saw the curtained posts of the massive bed in which she had been sleeping.

She slowly sat up, stretching and taking in her surroundings. The room was bathed in the afternoon sun, and was more impressive in daylight where one could more fully appreciate the antique furnishings and other rich milieus. Judging by the satisfied ache in her muscles, she had slept long enough…although in this lush environment, she could have easily hibernated until summer.

Moving to the gilded antique vanity mirror, she gave her reflection a cursory glance, briefly attempting to tame her riot of red curls, a curse she had battled since she was a child. With an exasperated sigh, Maggie rolled her eyes and rubbed her face, resigning herself to the fact that on this day, she would allow her hair the freedom of being untethered, stemming more from a lack of energy to fight with it than from the decision that it was in any way desirable to her. She made her way to the bedroom door and stepped out into the hallway.

Descending the stairs, Maggie could hear a deep voice alternating with a hearty chuckle emanating from the bowels of the house; at least that's what it sounded like. The voices spoke in a rich tongue, and as she reached the bottom of the staircase and headed toward the kitchen, they became louder and clearer. Rounding the corner, she arrived at the source and discovered that it was Shannon exchanging jokes, and punches, with John.

"What's the difference between an Irish wedding and an Irish wake, mate?" she heard Shannon query as she entered. Approaching the duo, she could see John thoughtfully contemplating the riddle.

His coy grin indicated that he wasn't really sure, yet it didn't keep him from answering. "One person wishes they were dead, and the other one is?"

This elicited a grand round of laughs, and it was obvious to Maggie that the two had already drank quite a bit. Her suspicions were confirmed when she caught the strong scent of whiskey wafting from their general direction.

"No!" Shannon managed to squeak out, after catching his breath from the laughs racking his chest and abdomen. "There's one less drunk, there is!" His answer elicited another wave of raucous laughter that was contagious, and Maggie found herself giggling along with them.

When the two men noticed her, they nodded in her direction, acknowledging her. John poured another drink for them. "Will ye have a glass with us, lassie?" Shannon asked Maggie, holding up his own to her in inquiry.

She stared at it for a moment, considering her plans for the day. Deciding that she may as well enjoy her time away from work since the passing of her mother, Maggie accepted Shannon's offer. She didn't fail to notice the large grin that spread across Shannon's face, splitting it in two. Once filled half-way up, the three clinked their glasses together and up-ended the contents into their awaiting gullets.

Maggie immediately felt her face become flushed, along with the pleasant burn in her tummy that always accompanied a shot of whiskey for her. When the contents of her glass were empty, she looked up and realized that both men were staring, appraising her.

"Ye got some Irish blood, do ya?" Shannon asked, the smile remaining on his face. John obviously interpreted his statement as a request for more and happily obliged, refilling the three tumblers. Maggie returned Shannon's stare shyly, feeling as though he was looking into her soul. Suddenly, the spell was broken when John handed them each their drinks.

Feeling the cool glass in her palm, she studied the amber liquid, considering the man she had shared her bed with the day before. Though she had just met Shannon, she was becoming more attracted to him by the minute. In fact, she knew very little of him, but her ignorance was offset by her normally astute judgment of character. Smiling to herself, she decided that he was likely a good person and she wanted to get to know him better.

Her private musings were interrupted by John sharing a joke of his own. Maggie wondered if this was a game they played: a shared joke followed by tossing back a glass. "What did the drunk Irishman say to the drunk bloke that was stealin' his hooch?"

Shannon was quiet for a moment, a look of concentration plain on his face, obviously contemplating the answer to the riddle. Maggie, being not nearly as intoxicated, fixated on his facial expressions with interest. When it became clear that he could not come up with the answer, she piped up, "What did the drunk Irishman say to the drunk bloke that was stealin' his hooch," attempting to imitate the brogue as closely as her limited experience with the Irish lilt would allow.

Shannon blinked at her, agreeing, "Aye, that's the riddle, Lass." He then turned back to study John, whose face had broken into another wide grin as he watched Maggie. Realizing Shannon's confusion, John let out a hearty chuckle and informed him, "The girl is not nearly as thick-skulled as you, my old friend."

Maggie couldn't help but laugh with John, to Shannon's dismay. After darting glances back and forth between the two of their guffawing faces, he slapped himself in the head and laughed along with them. "Aye, she is not at that!" he agreed, finally catching the joke. Chuckling heartily, he raised his glass in a toast, prompting the other two to join him, upending their drinks in unison.

Once the containers were drained, the two men looked at Maggie expectantly. Baffled by their stares, her face reddened, and she looked at them askance. "It's ye're turn, love," Shannon informed her. She blinked at him until comprehension finally dawned.

Racking her brain in search of a joke, she finally offered, "Okay, how do you get a redhead to argue with you?" As soon as the words had left her mouth, the eyes of both men ascended to her disarray of crimson hair. John's mouth turned up slightly at the corner, and Shannon's face turned a darker shade of red as he watched her, considering her riddle. "Er, ye tell the wee lass that men are the brighter sex?"

Maggie's face turned an angry red, an automatic reaction to his sexist comment. Infuriated as she was at his misogynist remark, she was tempted to stomp on his foot. However, considering the answer to the riddle, she scowled at him, and then revealed the answer.

"No. You say…something," Maggie told him, staring him in the eye as if daring him to make another rude comment. Though she was generally very irritated by sexist comments and behavior, the broad, good-natured grin that broke out on Shannon's face, followed by his gales of laughter, had her smiling at him. Noting John's embarrassed grimace, which she figured was probably an attempt to hide his amusement, she decided that he was smarter than his friend, and likely had more training in the art of the avoidance of insulting women.

Her amusement was interrupted by Morgan entering the kitchen. "Sounds like a bunch of monkeys in here," she commented, smiling, and kissing John passionately on the lips. He pulled her into him and the two appeared lost in each other for the moment, oblivious to the world around them.

When the silence became awkward for the two left out of the intimate embrace, Shannon refilled the whiskey glasses. *"Ahem!"* Shannon cleared his throat before continuing. A bit louder, he offered, "Would ye like to have a spot o' whiskey, little miss?"

At this, the lovers finally looked up. With a quick shake of the head, Morgan answered, "No. I've never really had a taste for it. But I'd love some Captain Morgan, if you have some, John," she requested, gazing at John suggestively.

John moved away from the counter he had been leaning against, and taking her by the hand, walked through the kitchen door with Morgan in tow, leaving Shannon and Maggie alone.

Staring at each other in the awkward way of lovers who had experienced each other sexually but knew little else of the other, the silence stretched. It was broken by Maggie clearing her throat. "Shall we try for another round?" she asked him.

He jumped, startled as if goosed from behind. Hiding his embarrassment, he grabbed the bottle swiftly, pouring them each a nearly full glass.

"I say we just sip it this time. I canna come up with any jokes I would deem appropriate for yer ears at the present moment," he explained. She obediently sipped, the room falling into uncomfortable silence.

Eventually, motivated by her liquid courage, Maggie asked, "So you're from Ireland, like John?" After his brief nod she continued, "Do you have any one special in your life? A misses Shannon?"

He choked on his whiskey at the sudden turn of conversation, and Maggie had to pound him on the back to assure he was moving oxygen effectively into his lungs again. Finally, with a reddened face, he answered, "Nay. That is...well...me wife, though a bonnie lass, was also found to be quite bonnie by some other bastards, and...well...wife is a right nicer term fer her than I would choose ter call her at the present moment." He finished his explanation bitterly, downing the rest of his alcohol.

Maggie noted his cynical smile, but sensed a hint of sadness as well. His expression quickly turned sour then, and he added angrily, "It's no matter though. I'm no needin' to be tied just at the moment to anyone, and besides, who really wants ter father a bastard child; she told me, she did, tha' she ha' been pregnant many times over the years. I couldna ever even say for sure that they was mine." Introspectively, he added quietly, "No tha' it matters, since she saw fit to get rid o' the wee ones early on without ever telling me."

Maggie regretted bringing up the subject; it made her feel uncomfortable, and as though she was getting more of a glimpse into Shannon than he would have chosen to reveal if he had been sober. In an attempt to lighten the mood, she grabbed the whiskey bottle from behind him and refilled their tumblers. Handing his to him, she raised her glass and confidently declared, "To not being tied down to worthless asses!" He touched her glass with his and with a nod of agreement, downed it in one gulp.

"Aye, that is a worthwhile toast," he concurred. Maggie drained her own glass a moment later, and Shannon took his turn refilling them. "How 'bout you lassie? Anyone special ye're attached to?"

Maggie had brought the rim of the glass to her lips, but at his query, pulled it back, and staring into space, mused, "Mmmmm, not currently." Bringing her eyes to meet his, she stated, "My mom, you see, she was very ill for a long time."

As Shannon's expression became confused, she elaborated. "You see, my mom has lived with me for the last few years and I took care of her. I'm a nurse, and the type of medical care she needed would have been very expensive, had she been hospitalized." She quickly caught her mistake and wanted to correct herself to include the fact that her mom had just passed, but his perplexed look persisted, so she continued. "Well, most guys, at least the ones I've gone out with, don't stick around very long after they find out about my decrepit mother living with me."

Shannon's expression conveyed understanding which quickly changed to indignation as he exclaimed, "What kinda silly hog swallop is that? Ye mean ye were caring for yer mum an' it made the boys not interested in ye?" When Maggie nodded, he continued, "Tha's daft! What do the wee knuckle heads be thinkin'? If they were to mate yer, they'd be lucky, cuz then ye'd be more likely ter be carin' fer the likes of them when they get to passin'. An' correct me if I'm wrong, as I've got no medical knowledge to speak of, but don' women outlive men by plenty these days?"

Maggie watched him silently, fascinated, as his accent thickened in his worked up state. She couldn't help but smile, wondering if Irish culture was in general that much different than American culture.

"Well, it certainly has made the prospect of dating disappointing," Maggie admitted, as she sipped her whiskey. Absently, she remarked, "I've kinda sworn off men for the time being, in fact. It's just gotten too hard to handle the repeated rejection once I tell them about my mom." Looking into his face she confessed with a bitter smile, "I'd actually gotten into the habit of telling them from the outset of my mom's illness, just to head off the chance of getting to know them better. It's amazing how quickly they hit the road sometimes, and how easily you can read their expressions when they're deciding that they want nothing to do with a chick that cares for a helpless patient full time."

Shannon's eyes became somewhat distant and Maggie figured that despite his condemnation of the men she had dated, he was probably thinking how he, too, would have escaped, had he found himself in that position with her. Wanting to drown the hurt from her painfully persistent memories of rejection, she took several large gulps, emptying her glass.

After several moments of companionable silence, his eyes adjusting, he looked at her dry cup, and grabbed for the bottle. Then, as if reconsidering, his hand stilled, wrapping around it as he studied her face. "Would ye like to have a sit down fer a moment, lass?"

She looked up at him, realizing that she was well on her way to being drunk, and smiled contently.

Straightening himself to his full height, Shannon started for John's office, which currently served as his makeshift guest room. He moved slowly; tentatively. Likely so that she could accompany him. When she began walking, her knees weakened from so much alcohol in such a short period of time. Stepping back suddenly, he wrapped his arm around her waist, steadying her. Maggie enjoyed his solid presence and his strength, wondering if he too cherished her being there.

He was tall, as was she, but he still dwarfed her. She felt that they fit nicely together…especially when her careless footing nearly caused her to topple over. He saved her, swiftly grabbing and righting her, pulling her into him more firmly. Maggie smiled shyly up at him, leaning heavily into him. More to feel his hard body than to lean on his strength.

As they entered the study, Shannon helped Maggie to the couch. Sitting next to her, he poured himself more whiskey. Her glass was empty, as was her chest, and she planned to remedy both problems. Lifting her glass close to his face, she gave a silent bid for more.

Turning to her, he appeared mildly surprised that she would want to be more intoxicated than her present drunkenness already allowed. "Want some more do ye? I don't suppose ye've got Scottish or Irish blood in ye, the way ye throw back the whiskey, lass?"

Glass satisfactorily filled, she emptied it in a quick burning swallow. Considering her ignorance of the answer to his question, she felt embarrassed for a moment, but then replied, "I don't really know, actually."

His puzzled look prompted her to continue. "I've never met my father. It was always just me and my mom."

She wasn't sure how he'd take her admission, since often when she had made it, she was promptly treated by many men as diseased, or like she had the Ebola virus. At this point of intoxication, however, she was past the point of caring, and would no longer keep her dirty secrets hidden in hopes of avoiding rejection. Somewhere, something within her had changed. Her mother's death, followed by empty sex with the doctor, reminiscent of the endless meaningless dates with anonymous superficial jerks…somewhere warped in those events she had finally decided that she would no longer hide that which she had no control over. Nor did she any longer care what others thought of it.

At this point, she made a snap decision. Fueled by her newfound motivation, mingled with a deep-seeded anger stemming from her past experiences, she decided that she was going to in fact become heavily inebriated; also that she wanted the sizeable man sitting next to her to be inside of her again. However, considering her scant experience with flirtation, she cursed her naive skills of seduction.

Taking the plunge, she decided to go after what she wanted, consequences be damned. Boldly placing her hand on his thigh palm down, she smiled at him, holding the tumbler out for more whiskey.

Shannon had been watching her, his look of surprise changing to one of concern. Taking the glass from her, he set the bottle down, placing her glass on the floor next to it. "I think ye've had enough for a time, lassie," he cautioned, looking down at her. This prompted her to cross her arms over her chest and pout like a petulant child.

She felt her face begin to redden in the process, comprehending that she was being unreasonable. Further, his mouth curved up in one corner while he worked to console her with a lopsided smile. "It's not that I terribly mind if ye get drunk, ye see, I jus' want ye not ter do it so bloody fast." He seemed to think he was being very reasonable and looking out for her best interests, but his patronizing tone and solid reasoning only infuriated her further.

He continued to watch her face silently and carefully, as if she were a ticking time bomb. She was becoming angrier by the second, as though coiled and ready to strike, although she kept her eyes trained on the floor at her feet. She knew her face must match the hues of her crimson hair, and she couldn't seem to control her frantically twitching foot as she sat next to him and the tension continued to build. Her nervous energy was soon rising out of control and she had to move, or else she felt sure her head would explode.

Suddenly, she jumped up off of the couch as though something had bitten her, and began pacing the room like a caged animal. Noticing his confusion, she thought it likely that he couldn't discern the source of her agitation, though he seemed fascinated by her pacing movements as he tracked her back and forth across the room.

Finally, she stopped in front of him, looking down at him and taking her turn to study him. The two silently watched each other, Shannon tensing. He tentatively reached for her hand as if he had a compulsion to touch her. Maggie wondered if he felt the same as she…that if they didn't touch…communicate physically in some way…the tension would become so much that one of them would soon break.

He hesitated as the gap closed between them, until finally he grabbed her by the hand, pulling her onto his lap.

As they connected…he reaching out to her, and she allowing herself to be captured by him…Shannon felt something change within himself. As the two collided, it was as though this moment had been destined since the beginning of time, and to him, it felt like everything fell into place.

Maggie landed on Shannon with a muffled groan while he looked into her eyes and saw something that he recognized very well, for he had seen it in himself every day since his wife had left. He saw vulnerability there, and hunger; for the touch of another human being, and for the primal contact that was so basic to the health and happiness of all living creatures.

He brought his hand to her face, caressing her cheek. After staring at her lips for what seemed like an eternity, he pulled her to him, capturing her mouth. She returned his affection and they devoured each other while their hands roamed, exploring, and undressing the other.

When he had her clothing fully removed, he was still dressed below the waist, and he worked to correct it, lying her on the couch next to him. She did not cooperate with him, however, holding his face to hers while her fingertips wandered from his shoulders and his chest, down to the front of his jeans.

"Hurry up and take them off," she demanded in a husky whisper. He happily obliged and was rewarded with her pulling his hips toward her moist core, wrapping her legs around him.

He entered Maggie with such force that he was concerned he might have hurt her. However, looking at her face, he could see that the moans that escaped from her quivering lips were from pleasure and not pain. He continued to repeat the cycle of driving into her and then retreating. Before he could stop himself, his release spewed out of him while he moaned loudly into her hair, collapsing on top of her.

He hated that he had climaxed so quickly, but her legs and arms wrapped so tightly around him, coupled with her moans told him that she was not upset with what had transpired. After catching his breath, he lifted himself up to rest his weight on his elbows, turning his face into her neck, and inhaling her clean scent of sweat that had broken out there. Smiling to himself, he realized that her perspiration smelled of whiskey.

After lying together attached for a while, she turned her face into his and captured his lips. They kissed then, more deeply than their earlier impassioned foreplay…but the end result was the same, and they were both quickly breathing heavily.

Shannon wanted her again, and his hand ascended from where it rested on her hip to lay on her heaving breast. Cupping it, he teased her nipple with his thumb, causing her to moan from the pleasure he was creating. Soon she was moving her hips into him again, and the hot wet friction caused him to become erect.

After moving into each other several times, Maggie placed her hand on his chest, prompting him to stop. "I want more of you," she announced, searching his face. In a gesture that took in her body where he was lodged within her, she stated, "In here...I want you deeper."

He considered her words for a moment while studying her. The expressions that chased across her face suggested that she thought she had ruined the moment by asking him for more. Not wanting to disappoint, he repositioned himself in front of the couch on his knees, moving her legs so that her calves rested on his chest and her heels were hooked, lying over his shoulders.

Before he thrust himself forward, he stared down at her face for a moment and caressed her legs, appreciating the muscular grace and the long form of them. "Are ye ready for me to be buried deep in ye, love?" he entreated her. Her eyes hadn't left his face as she watched him appraising her, naked and vulnerable, laid out in front of him. Finally, in silent acquiescence, she gave a slight nod. He entered her with a force and a thoroughness that had him buried like a sword to the hilt.

Maggie moaned as her hips moved to meet his assault. Continuing their erotic dance, they joined together again and again, until she cried out with a loud moan that echoed within the confines of the room.

She then fell back, completely limp, with a happily relaxed expression on her face. Shannon continued to piston into her until his orgasm spewed into her, and then collapsed on top of her again. He was worried that he was crushing her, but her arms held him to her, so he rested on top of her, trying to catch his breath.

As they lay together, working to regulate their breathing, Shannon was again inhaling the clean scent that emanated from her neck. Maggie was staring blankly above her, a large grin plastered on her face. She looked utterly satisfied and content, and Shannon basked in the joy that seemed to emanate from her, elated; he couldn't remember the last time he had felt so fully sated after making love. They basked in each other's presence; neither moved, likely fearing that the magic moment would be over too soon.

****

Morgan followed John into the small room to the side of the home's entryway in search of her favorite rum. Upon entering, she realized that it was the same place they had confessed their tryst to John's wife, Jasmine the week before.

Reflecting on the events of the last several days, she mused that her life had turned around dramatically over the course of a scant few weeks. Before entering the short-lived affair with the married couple, Morgan had been happily single, cherishing her fierce independence. She couldn't even imagine falling in love, let alone entering into a relationship; at least before she got to know John's love for her and his passion. Making love to him was the most intense experience she'd ever been through, and she couldn't even fathom the idea of being without it at this point.

After entering the room, John shut the door behind them, pulling her from her reverie and closing them in intimately. Morgan was standing in front of the liquor cabinet, perusing the contents when John stepped up behind her, embracing her. She absorbed his heat and the strength of his arms as he pulled her into him.

"Mmmmm," John breathed into her neck, taking her scent into his lungs. She leaned into him and could feel his burgeoning erection pushing into the padding of her buttocks. She smiled to herself, wiggling her bottom and stoking the fire building in his shaft.

"Mmmmm. You're right," she teased, imitating his pleasured sigh, and then joked, "you have Captain Morgan Black." There was a pause as she awaited his response…it came in the form of him pinching her budding nipple.

When he spoke to her next, she could feel his breath right up against her skin as he said with a nibble of her ear, "Is that all that you are finding to be desirable, *ma shearc*?" As he said this, he pulled her more firmly into him with one hand and increased the pressure on her nipple with the other.

"That and the crushed ice," she said with a smile in her voice, as she brought his fingers to her mouth and bit down, punishing him for his recent retaliatory squeeze.

She waited for him to react as she swirled her tongue over the marks on his fingers. For a moment nothing happened and she wondered if he'd heard her. Next, she wondered if he was letting her get away with it.

When she felt his mouth at her neck, she knew she was in for something delicious, thanks to John's need to exact his sweet revenge on perceived slights. As the pressure increased, he pulled her backwards, stopping abruptly at the sofa and descending, pulling her onto his lap.

As his fingers found their way through the myriad of fabric into the maze of robe, night gown, and panty, he breathed in her ear, "Is that so? There is nothing else here that you desire?" At the end of his query he arrived at his destination and dipped his fingers in, sampling the wetness she released at his insistence. He then massaged a circle with his fingertips, causing her to move and moan in his arms. He increased pressure until her breath escaped in gasps, her body shuddering on his lap.

Finally he asked again, "What else would you like me to do to you my love?" He did not cease his assault of her, and she was moving back and forth on him, causing his shaft to grow larger. Morgan worried he would burst with wanting her, and knew that he needed to find release.

She grasped his free hand that had been resting on her hip, pulling it desperately to her mouth. She then captured it, nearly sucking his fingers down her throat. As much as he likely wanted her to feel a suspenseful and pleasurable sensation before he brought her to climax, the pressure that he felt from her seductive movements had reached its brink and he was beginning to become desperate for a release.

He pushed her off of his lap so that she found herself lying on the sofa, and with satisfaction, she readied herself for him as he tore at his clothing to remove barriers. With a ball-slapping force, he entered her while she watched him through half-lidded eyes.

After several rapid, forceful cycles in and out of her that effectively dispelled some of the building pressure, he slowed, watching her face. The blissful smile he saw there had him reaching down and sampling her lips. She returned his passion, and though he had stilled himself to savor the taste of her, he was becoming breathless again. Realizing this, he came to the conclusion that she was as well.

He could have gone on kissing her all afternoon, though the pressure in his groin was beginning to build to a fever pitch again. Still, he wanted to savor what his mouth tasted. When she began thrusting her hips up to meet his, pleading with him to continue his work, he removed his lips from her and then, using his hold on her hips to gain purchase, he began pounding into her again.

Her hands gripping his arms and her moaning told him that she was in as much bliss as he, and he thought for a moment to draw it out in reparation for her earlier misbehavior. However, he could no longer hold back, and found himself working hard to finish what he had started.

"Oh John," she nearly yelled, in a frenzy that only he could remedy. He was still tempted to tease her and keep that which she so deeply desired just out of her reach by slowing to a snail's pace. Unfortunately, his body had demands of its own, and as she arched into him with her mouth wide open, and a silent shout on her tongue, his hips moved of their own volition and he cried out, spending himself into her. Unable to move more than scant inches to allow himself to breathe, he turned his face to her and took in the clean scent of her freshly washed hair. The two lovers then lay, hooked together, in peaceful bliss, until sleep overtook them.

Chapter Two

As Jasmine awakened from her afternoon nap, she noted the rapidly disappearing light that streamed through the wooden blinds with a start. "The children!" she exclaimed, when she saw Patrick's questioning glance.

"Me mum is caring for them, *a ghra mo chroi*." He said this while rubbing the stubble of his chin on her neck. Though it was scratchy to the delicate skin there, she snuggled into him instead of pulling away. He finished his explanation, stating, "I looked in on the wee ones this morning when I went to get coffee and asked me mum to watch after them so we could work things out."

Jasmine suddenly sat up, moving away from him, alarmed and asked, "What did you tell her, Patrick?" He smiled at her for a moment and then pulled her into him once more and assured, "I told me mum like this," he wiggled his eyebrows at her, continuing, "me woman needs a little bedding time wi' her man, Mum! Can ye keep an eye on the babbies so I can service her right an' good?"

Her face blushed bright red and she pulled away from him again, accentuating her actions with a hard smack on his chest. "Patrick, you didn't!" she exclaimed. His face reddened as he considered her expression, though it wasn't from embarrassment. He was working at holding his laugh in at the shock he had just given her. Finally, when her lip quivered, and he thought the tears might start, he embraced her stiff form and pulled her onto his lap, despite her resistance. "I was just teasin' ya know."

He kissed her lips, which were becoming more pliant by the moment, chuckling heartily into her neck, as she attempted to move away from him in response to his verbalized amusement. "Ye should've seen your face, love; it was red as summer sunset."

Ceasing her struggling movements, she looked at his face curiously and asked, "Patrick, what is…ah hraw…muh hurry? Is that the right way to say it?" She waited, wide-eyed for his explanation as he stared at her, seeming to study her forever. Finally, his lips quirked in a secret smile and he drew her in, kissing her forehead.

He moved down her face to her lips, becoming more impassioned, until he needed more and his hand descended from her face to rest between her legs. He rubbed her with his fingers, and then smiled widely at her and said, "Aye, you're so wet and ready for me." She moved into his hand at his words. In one swift movement he moved her from sitting on his lap to lying her on her back, parting her thighs with his body. She moaned, breathless, and her hips started a slow erotic dance, bucking into him, as though her body had a mind of its own and wanted to seduce his.

When he was about to enter her, she pulled back, making him wait for what he so badly wanted. In his present state, he was in her control, ready to do whatever she wanted so that he could have her. He looked her in the eye, awaiting direction as to how she wanted him to take her.

"I want to be on top of you," she instructed, adding, "pinch my nipples while I ride you," as she straddled him.

He complied during their slow and sensuous ride. He watched her face as she moved back and forth on top of him. When she moaned quietly with her eyes closed, he knew that she was in a state of sexual bliss. Looking up at her where his fingers squeezed her, he increased the pressure until her moans became louder, the pumping of her hips increasing in urgency.

As she rode him, he had to close his eyes to absorb the sensations, though he continued to tweak her nipples. Suddenly, after moving frantically, she arched her back and then froze in an orgasmic fixed position. He knew she had climaxed because he could feel her wetness bathing him. Needing to achieve his own orgasm, he prompted her to roll over and then pounded into her.

She watched him through half-lidded eyes. He knew that she loved to watch him when he moved inside her, loved the changing expressions on her face. He imagined that unlike the sex she had always had with his brother, when her beloved was moving inside of her after she orgasmed, the pleasure he enjoyed gave her great pleasure.

As he continued to move inside her, she began to moan again, as he knew he was stimulating her most sensitive spots. "Mmmmm, Jasmine, you are so hot and wet for me," he managed to sputter out through gritted teeth. Her hips bucked, meeting his thrusts, until finally they both came together, calling each other's names.

Lying skin to skin, they kissed and embraced each other, then snuggled together and fell asleep in each other's arms. Sometime later, Patrick reached for a quilt and covered the two of them, enveloping them in a blissful warmth as they napped together.

****

As Siobhan Kelly turned her key in the lock, she was mildly surprised that it still worked. Shannon hadn't been in his pub downstairs; or at least he hadn't been visible behind the bar... not even after she had spied upon the establishment for several minutes. Knowing her husband, if he was there, he'd be in the middle of the crowd, giving out advice, or singing and drawing the people to him in some way. Rolling her eyes at the thought of her gregarious spouse, she ascended the stairs. She had never liked all of the attention he constantly paid to his patrons which took up so much of his time and left so little of his affections for her.

When she entered their apartment, she was surprised yet again: he was nowhere to be found. Looking around and noting the disheveled clothes and drawers hanging out, her mind began working. She crossed the kitchen and pulled out the drawer closest to the Frigidaire.

Sure enough, on the pad he kept there for scribbling notes when taking phone messages, she saw flight information. Noting the date and time, it seemed he had left abruptly two days before her arrival.

Her heart sank. How could he just up and leave her? Especially when she had, against her better judgment, come back to him. Every time before when she had left him, upon returning he'd be waiting for her, often begging if she put on a show of being reluctant about staying.

Admittedly, she had been crueler this time, even confessing some of the abortions she had gotten during the course of their marriage. She hadn't even told him about all of them, but she knew that hearing it had hurt him by the look he wore and the tears he had shed. It had also made him extremely angry, and she had thought for a moment that he was going to strike her, though that hadn't stopped her from rubbing his nose in it.

Looking back, she figured that his punching the wall was the only thing that kept him from punching her. She studied the wall next to their bedroom door as these thoughts ran through her mind. It was a sizeable hole that caused her to smile for a moment, considering the fool she had married. Walking into her bedroom, she saw that her things were still neatly folded in her drawer and she had to smile to herself again. She would get him back, and eventually he would beg her.

Pulling out her cell phone, she called him. When it went straight to voice mail, she was surprised, but not discouraged. When she was able, she left a message for her husband, "Shannon…" she said in the most pathetic voice she could muster, "I came home. I really missed ye and…wanted ter talk things over with ye…Give me a call. Ye know the number. And Shannon…I miss ye terrerbly. Please call me." Hanging up the phone, she smiled to herself. Her acting performance had almost brought tears to her own eyes, she had been so convincing.

Her next task was to charm the pub staff so that they felt sorry for her and would sympathize with her. That would move them to work with her to get Shannon to come back to her. His flight looked like he had taken a trip to The States, so he wouldn't be back any time soon. This gave her plenty of time to strategize. By the time he landed safely back on Irish soil, his employees would be pissed at him if he didn't take her back. Smiling to herself, she exited through the door which she had entered less than ten minutes earlier, heading toward the pub to put her scheme to work.

****

After David hung up on the white trash he had fucked, his anger boiled over and he slammed the receiver against the wall several times. More than anything, he wanted to break something or hurt someone. He had been able to keep his cool while he was on the phone with the little cunt, but he knew that had she been there, he would've hurt her badly. He knew it because it wasn't the first time he'd seen red when he was furious, and his rage felt impotent until he was able to spend it on an object, or preferably a person.

Get yourself together, he told himself. A man in his position had to maintain control above all else at all times. He sucked in a few deep breaths and blew them through his lips slowly. He had managed to keep his temper reigned in for so long, but when little whores had the nerve to call him up out of the blue and threaten him, he had difficulty not losing it. Just then a thought occurred to him as a sinister smile curled his lips.

The slut that had just contacted him was upset because she had seen him kiss one of his patient's family members in the hall. It was likely that the bitch was jealous because she was desperate to get what he could offer. As a neurology Fellow…a respected physician…he had a lot going for him. That and his prominent family, who was more than willing to clean up after his little indiscretions. Like the one that could have ended his medical career at the end of his fourth year of medical school.

That fucking bitch had been asking for it, and he had given it to her in the form of the beating of her life right after he screwed her drunk ass so hard she had bled all over him. Between the ass fucking and the beating he had given her, she probably hadn't walked straight for a month. He snickered to himself as he remembered her face plastered on the front page of the newspaper. He wouldn't have recognized her had he not seen his own handy work just after he'd done it. And luckily, the greedy little whore had taken the lump sum of cash his family had offered. Truthfully, he couldn't blame her. Had his lawyers had their day in court to play with her, she would've ended up looking like the loosest street walker to ever stand on a corner, he pictured with a sinister smile.

It just went to show that whores could be bought, and in his mind they were all whores. It was just a matter of hooking them before treating them as their real nature deserved. Once they were hooked, he could do whatever he wanted with them; this almost always meant treating them like his property, which is what they were ultimately.

David spent the next thirty seconds planning his revenge on the cunt-bitch nurse's aide that deserved to be punished. She should've considered herself lucky that his dick had cared to grace her pussy with its presence. Instead, she was calling him to complain about him not calling her back. As if someone like her had any chance with him. When a CNA fucked a neurology Fellow in the medicine room at the hospital, did she really think she was girlfriend material? He scoffed at the idea, and then smiled at his plan to make her want to quit. He was about to make her life a living hell.

Chapter Three

Maggie awakened nude in Shannon's arms. As she lifted the blanket, she discovered that he, too, was naked. Looking over at the clock, she saw that it was 9 p.m. and was surprised to realize that they had slept, cocooned together, for several hours.

She looked over at him, studying his peacefully sleeping features. His hair was also red, but not quite as bright a hue as hers. He had a thin sprinkling of freckles that ran from cheek to nose to cheek, which she found quite appealing. She could see laugh lines around his mouth and remembered his boisterous chuckle. She thought that he was probably generally good-natured. He had a five o'clock shadow, and she wondered when he had shaved last, or if he was the type that normally went shaggy.

Observing other areas of his anatomy, she noticed stickiness where their skin touched. Maggie thought it likely that it was from the two of them sweating during their earlier arduous activities. Though she would ordinarily find that disgusting, like the sweaty skin of her dirty patients, she found that she didn't mind being sweaty with Shannon. On the contrary, the thought actually turned her on.

Silently musing over what the two of them had been doing together, Maggie remembered the feel of Shannon deep inside her, and wanted to see him again. Glancing at his face to ensure that he remained asleep, she carefully lifted the blanket, stealing a peek. His pubic region was covered with a rich carpet of red curly hairs that corkscrewed over his mons pubis. Just below the area that contained the thickest covering, his sex organ dominated so that she could scarcely see his scrotum peeking out on either side.

A throaty sound had her turning her head to look at his face, and she saw that he was watching her. "Ye like what ye see, do ya?" he asked with a cocky grin.

She dropped the blanket, lying back and covering her eyes with her hand. She could feel her face turning bright red as it burned with embarrassment.

Shannon chuckled, unashamed of his nudity. He then grabbed her at her ribs and teased, whispering in her ear, "All ye have to do is ask, love…but fair is fair, and I want to look at you, too."

His statement caused Maggie to erupt into a volley of giggles as she turned her head in an attempt to hide her face. Obviously encouraged, he threw the blanket away from their bodies so that it landed on the floor, moving to straddle one of her thighs. She resisted, attempting to hold her legs together. Shannon laughed, mischievously tickling her inner thighs and working to coax them open, reminding her, "Now love, ye got to take a look; I just want the same thing fer meself."

Giggling and squirming, she turned her face away from the pillow and looked at him. "You really want to look at me down there?" she asked.

He smiled down at her, assuring, "Mmmmm. More than anathing, love. And I want to taste ye right here." He said this as he fondled her between her legs, causing her to arch into his fingertips. Already slick where he touched her, he dipped his fingers in and then brought them to his mouth, making heavy eye contact. "Ye taste good, and ye're makin' me mouth water to have ye're flavor on me tongue." With that, he brought his mouth to her core and swirled an erotic massage.

As he lapped at her, he thrusted into her deeper and deeper with his fingers, stimulating her sensitive nerve endings. Quickly, he had her moaning and writhing; in a thrall from his sensual ministrations. She was moving frantically from the gathering pleasure he was creating, and he was becoming frenzied from his luscious feeding. Soon, his chin and cheeks were covered in the ambrosia she created.

Shannon appeared wrapped up in his task, but soon paused for air. When he did, he exclaimed through gritted teeth, "Fuck, Maggie, ye're so bloody hot!" He continued to plunge into her with his fingers. When his mouth descended on her again, he swirled his tongue on her erect nub, quickly increasing the pressure there until she exploded into his mouth, her eyes glazing over.

He had to know that the sensations he was creating were intense. Maggie moaned and bucked, wrapping her thighs around his neck and arching her back off of the couch, remaining affixed to his mouth. Soon, he replaced his fingers with his tongue, stabbing the soft tip as deep as it would go, as if working to extract as much of her sweet essence as possible.

Finally, he must have had enough, and his sensual massage ceased. Shannon gradually released the hold he had on her with his mouth and allowed her to settle onto the couch. Where she was lying against him, Maggie could feel his engorged shaft pressing against her leg. She knew that the pressure there must be overwhelming, just as the pleasure he'd just doled out had overwhelmed her. It was confirmed as she gazed up at him, a fevered expression on his face. As her hands roamed his body, he firmly grasped her hips with both hands, in a hurry to be inside her.

Using her hips to gain purchase, he entered her with a force that pushed her head against the cushy arm of the couch. Though Maggie had just orgasmed, Shannon was building her up again, pistoning into her at the perfect tempo. Each of his thrusts created bursts of pleasure in exactly the right spot, Maggie riding these waves of ecstasy until she was pushed over the edge. Gloriously, she orgasmed, gripping his shoulder and pulling him closer to her.

Maggie couldn't see his face, only his neck, but she had no doubt that he was close to the apex as his movements became more frantic. Closing her eyes, she savored the sensation, feeling every inch of him as he moved inside her. She yearned for him to reach his climax as she so desperately wanted to return to him the gift that she had just experienced.

Fisting her fingers in his hair in a fit of passion, she held him close to her. Short, grunty sounds escaped his throat as his hips rocked back and forth. Frantically he moved. Faster and faster until finally, with a final vigorous thrust, he exploded inside of her. The sudden torrent of wetness was unmistakable as his seed spewed into her.

Shannon collapsed on top of her, the two locked together, motionless, except for their chests heaving in exhaustion as they worked to catch their breath. They remained this way for several moments, spent from their strenuous workout.

The silence was broken when Shannon laughed, prompting Maggie to inquire into his chest. "What's so funny, honey?" He bent down to kiss her forehead, swiping at the stray damp hairs that had stuck to it.

"I was just thinking that this is the most enjoyable workout I've had in a long time, and if this could be me exercise I would ha' no problem doin' it every day. In fact, I'd pro'ly do it religiously!" This elicited giggles from Maggie. As she laughed, merriment further lightening her mood, Shannon watched her, appearing happy and content. "Come here, you," he told her, pulling her face to his. He kissed her forehead first, but then moved his lips down her face, stopping at her nose and then her cheeks. Eventually he reached her lips, which he thoroughly explored.

"Mmmmm," she sighed, between breathless kisses. "I like the shit out of kissing you." She could feel his forceful exhalation as he released her in order to make his own proclamation. "Me too, *mo ruin*," he concurred, before returning his lips to her luscious mouth. His hand continually caressed her face while holding her to him, enabling him to continue his exploration. During this erotic perusal of each other, Shannon parted Maggie's thighs with one knee so that she was straddling his leg. She took the opportunity to grind on him where he was pushed up against her inflamed nub.

As their mutual arousal increased, they thrust into each other, separated only by his phallus, which was becoming longer and harder by the minute. They breathed raggedly into each other as the pressure built, turning first into a dull roar, and then a conflagration that had each wanting to devour the other. Finally, Shannon shifted his weight and entered her. They both gasped, as much from the delicious pleasure the contact gave them, as from the sheer ecstasy of being joined again.

After shifting his weight, he was again on top of her, but didn't have much room to maneuver. After pumping into her a few times, he slowed, and then stopped, pivoting around so that he was on his knees in front of the couch. He then pulled her forward so that her bottom was perched at the edge, pounding into her again, eliciting several blissful moans.

Shannon had to know he was building an ecstatic fire for Maggie by the way her head tossed from side to side. Further, she clenched onto him desperately, as if he were her lifeline. As he continued to piston into her, their synchronous groans of desire became increasingly louder as the crescendo of pleasure grew. Maggie's grasp on Shannon's arms tightened until she nearly had a crushing grip. Finally she yelled out, "Oh my God!" as the powerful, throbbing orgasm ripped from her loins.

Shannon seemed exhilarated by her response, and it proved to be the boost that pushed him over the climactic edge as he exploded into her mere moments after her orgasm. Seemingly unable to hold himself up for another second, he collapsed on top of her, once again, spent from their vigorous carnal interlude.

Catching her breath and pinned contentedly beneath his weight, Maggie considered their recent trysts and couldn't help but smile. What she and Shannon had been doing was exquisite. If she was truthful with herself, she had to admit that it was the best she had ever had. In fact, the only time in her life another human being had brought her to orgasm were during her recent activities with him.

They lay together, attached for a few moments, until Shannon lifted himself up and announced, "I have need of the loo." Before he removed his body completely from hers, he leaned down and kissed her lips, slowly and sensually.

After he left, Maggie sat up and looked around for her clothes. With all of the sex they had recently had, she hadn't smoked since the day before, and she was in dire need of nicotine. She started to search for her purse, but quickly recalled that it was upstairs in the guest room where she had slept the first night.

When she opened the door to go retrieve her cigarettes, she found herself face to face with Shannon as he was returning to the study. When he looked at her quizzically, she explained her habit. "Aye, a cigarette is just what ye need after all that," he remarked with an unrepentant smile.

Maggie smiled shyly at his observation as he kissed her on the lips. "I can nay resist kissing ye're lips when ye smile at me tha' way," he whispered in her ear.

Had she not needed a cigarette so badly, Maggie would've followed him back into the study to resume their previous activities. It was with no small amount of determination that she headed toward her room after the passionate embrace they shared.

In the guest room, Maggie stood at the vanity, examining herself in the mirror. Studying her face, she saw that it glowed, and smiled brightly at her reflection, remembering her recent delectable events. Lifting her shirt, she looked at her breasts, noticing the small red marks around both of her nipples. She tweaked them to get an idea of how sore they were from where Shannon had enjoyed them. A small tingling, stinging sensation was the result, and her smile deepened as she ran her hands down her sides to assess for bruises and tenderness. Perusing her legs and the space between them, she finally decided she was satisfied with her bodily survey, and headed outside to smoke at long last.

Emerging from the warmth of the home, the outdoor air was crisp and the sky a smoky grey, promising more snow to come. Maggie nearly slipped on ice that looked deceptively like water, and had to throw out her hand to catch herself, her heartbeat quickening. She made swift work of smoking her first cigarette, lighting up another for good measure. If she and Shannon continued as previously, it could be quite a while before her next, she mused with a small giggle.

After finishing her "breathing treatment," as she jokingly referred to her habit, she collected her butts and went back into the house. In contrast to the frigid February air, the cozy heat was not unlike a blissful blanket enveloping her, a fire blazing in the living room's fireplace.

Entering the study, Shannon was on the phone in what sounded like quite a heated conversation. He angrily told the person on the other end of the line, "No ye don't, Siobhan. I donut want to see ye anymore. I told ya this already!"

He was silent for a moment, listening, as the person presumably responded to his statement. Continuing after a pause, he demanded, "Why in the good lord's name did ye go and do something like that, girl? I told ye I donut want to see ya, and there's nay ye can do about it. Not after everything ye've done… no, donut put Duncan on the phone. I donut need to speak with the chap, and he will nay change me mind." He breathed an exasperated sigh, shaking his head in frustration. Maggie was unsure if he was aware of her presence.

Sitting silently in the corner of the room, Maggie watched Shannon speak to this Duncan person, beginning to feel like an intruder. That is until he looked up at her with a brief smile, motioning for her to take a seat next to him. Standing at once, she went to him, holding the hand that he placed on her thigh.

With the phone to his ear, Shannon listened silently for a moment before grunting, "Aye, the diabolical wench is tryin' ter get ye to talk me into takin' er back but I canna do it, Duncan. Not after everythin' she ha' put me through. Wasting yer breath, ye are. I'll no have her back again."

Maggie swirled caresses on the back of Shannon's hand, working to comfort him. After a long moment of silence, he finally spoke. "Nay, Duncan, nay. I have nothing more ter say ter her… goodbye, me old friend, and *beannacht leat*." With this, Shannon snapped his phone shut and turned to Maggie. "Me wife, Siobhan," he explained. "She's tryin' ter get me ter take her back, the brasser."

Maggie reached across his lap and picked up the whiskey bottle from the floor. After taking a long swig from the bottle, she offered him a drink, which he gladly accepted. "Mmmmm, 'tis perfect fer drowning me sorrows, lass."

Maggie was taken aback by how long he swallowed as she watched him. She wasn't sure how he managed to go without breathing for so long. Finally, he lowered the bottle, letting out a soft belch. "Better out than in," he remarked, smiling ruefully at her.

Maggie reclaimed the bottle, taking another deep swallow, enjoying the accompanying burn, as she was still chilled from her venture outdoors. Once her thirst was quenched, she replaced the bottle on the floor. When she leaned across Shannon's legs, her breasts brushed against his thighs, sending little zings of pleasure through her. He apparently did not miss the feeling of her stiffening nipples rubbing against him, as he reached over, picking her up, and pulling her onto his lap.

"I'm right glad ye're here with me, lass," he told her before pulling her to him and gaining access to her neck. He took advantage of this and kissed her, lightly suckling her skin into his mouth. "Ye smell delicious *m' anam cara*, even though ye just lit up, and I love the way ye taste." She enjoyed the sensation of his mouth on her skin, leaning into him to increase the space he had access to.

"Mmmmm, Shannon, you feel so good to me." She turned to look at him as she made the statement. The slight movement caused his erection to rub against her bottom more vigorously, and her hand moved to cover it, as though it was on auto pilot.

His hips bucked, pushing his sex organ into her palm. Maggie smiled at him and announced, "Alright, fair is fair. Now it's my turn." He stared at her mutely for a moment, not comprehending her statement. When she stood up between his legs and faced him, understanding dawned. She kneeled between his legs and with a quick push, parted them, prompting him to remove his shorts.

When she made eye contact, she saw that he was studying her intently. She pointedly looked at his penis, making a show of slowly licking her lips. His cock jerked in reaction as much as in anticipation of the things she would do to him.

Maggie leaned forward and tentatively licked the mushroom head, swiping at it lightly. His hands fisted in her hair as he thrust into her mouth, forcing himself into the back of her throat. "Mmmmm, don't stop, cara," he managed to grit out between clenched teeth. Maggie enjoyed building the pleasure for him, increasing the suction as she took him over and over.

She watched his face, concentrating on her work and intent on the sensations she was creating. When he arched his back, the motion pushed his tip into her throat. She swallowed what he gave her, enjoying this newfound power while swirling her tongue rhythmically over his shaft. His hips began to move more frantically as he closed his eyes. She increased the pressure of the suction until he came with a force, spewing jets of hot semen into her throat. Wanting to finish what she had started, she continued to suck gently, draining every last drop, until his cock stopped jerking. She then released him, reseating herself in his lap. His arms settled around her limply as he laid his head back, smiling, in post-felatial bliss.

When he recovered, he repositioned her in his lap so that he could look at her. "I'll never look at yer lips the same again, *mo shearc*," he expressed, pulling her face to his and kissing the object of his affections.

Maggie returned his desire, and the two sat on the couch kissing until they were interrupted by John walking in. Fortunately, Maggie was dressed but Shannon was not, although her position on his lap effectively concealed his nudity.

"Oh, I didn't mean to interrupt," John started as he turned to make a hasty exit. He'd begun to leave, but on the threshold paused. Without turning to face the lovers, he announced, "Morgan just spoke with Lucia's nurse and she is being discharged at 9 a.m. tomorrow morning. Maggie, she was wondering if you would accompany her."

Maggie had to clear her throat, but then answered, "Of course. Tell her I'll be ready." John gave a slight nod of acknowledgment before closing the door behind him.

Shannon's hands began to roam her body again. Seeing the love bites he had made on her neck seemed to inspire him. "Would ye like ter have a bath with me, cara?"

Her face lit up at the prospect, and she stood up abruptly, bending over to pick up his shorts where they had been discarded onto the floor. "I would love to," she said, and then yelped as he smacked her bottom.

"I must warn ye that if ye bend over in front of me face like tha', I'll no resist the temptation to smack yer beautiful arse." Rubbing the spot where he had made contact, she smiled at him, and then said playfully, "Alright, happy hands, let's put those to good use for something other than spankings."

Shannon dressed himself before they made their way, hand in hand, to the guest room.

Upon arrival, he began the process of filling the tub while Maggie rummaged through her bags in search of a comfortable night gown. Locating the desired garb, she carried it into the bathroom and had to smile; Shannon was already in the tub and was singing. She thought it was probably in Gaelic, as she couldn't understand the words. He smiled back at her and held out his hand, beckoning her to join him.

When she had all of her clothing removed, she took his hand and stepped in carefully, foot between his thighs. The placement caused her ankle to brush up against his ball sack, which floated freely just above the floor of the tub. Shannon groaned lightly in response, but then continued singing, serenading Maggie, as he prompted her to sit on his lap. His voice was strong and beautiful, she noticed, as she lowered herself into the tub, relaxing against him. In a slow sultry movement, he brought his hands around and cupped her breasts, swirling circles over her nipples, which were already hardening into tight little buds.

As he finished his song, she was purring and content, turned on by his erotic massage. Turning her head to the side, he gained access to her mouth, placing kisses there, exploring, his tongue dipping in and out. He continued twirling his thumb over her right nipple with one hand as his other hand descended to massage the already sensitive bundle of nerves between her legs as well.

Maggie moaned into his mouth, becoming more breathless, until she finally cried out in a hoarse voice, "It's too much, Shannon. I need you inside me now!"

His arms tightened their hold on her as he grinned, whispering "Not yet. I've not had enough of feeling you jus' yet." He teased her, continuing the sensuous exploration of her body. Her hips were beginning to buck more wildly, and she wheezed in harsh gasps, as the waves of pleasure continued to overtake her.

"Please, Shannon! You're killing me! Put...your cock... inside me...now!" Maggie pleaded. He continued to make small circuits with his fingers for a moment longer, until finally he released her.

Lifting her slightly, he held her for several excruciatingly tense seconds, building the suspense while she wriggled around in an attempt to impale herself, wanting to dispel some of the building pressure. Finally, he pulled her onto him abruptly so that he entered her with a delicious force that had her crying out. The tub nearly full, it facilitated their continuous erotic cycle; one where he would rhythmically lift her, and then drop her onto him so that he impaled her deeply with his engorged shaft.

In the enclosed space, Maggie's cries of pleasure filled the room, and were soon joined by his. Finally, she orgasmed, rewarding Shannon with slick heat that helped him to climax with one last vigorous thrust inside her.

Spent, they leaned against the wall of the tub. Luckily, he had the wherewithal to turn off the water.

Shannon held her against him tightly as they breathed each other in for what seemed like an eternity. Finally, Maggie stirred, breaking the spell. Shannon gently turned her face toward his so that he could kiss her again. Regrettably, she halted this movement, stating, "Kissing you leads to other delicious things that distract me, and I need to get some sleep." He interrupted her with another thorough kiss that made her momentarily forget her goal. Giving in to his caresses, she allowed his touch, moving into his embrace. Closing her eyes and savoring the feel of his fingers on her face, she knew she could stay locked with him like this forever.

Suddenly, she pictured her best friend's face and her resolve returned. Maggie playfully bit Shannon's lip and then pushed on his chest. With a coy smile she teased, "You're trying to distract me again and I have to get up early in the morning."

He smiled at her wickedly, placing his hand between her thighs which caused her to moan. "That's right, cara, I like distracting you."

She removed his fingers from her core, pulling them to her mouth to suckle them. Smiling mischievously around them, she bit him lightly, causing him to pull his hand back, and feign injury.

"Don't be a baby," she admonished teasingly, and then reminded him, "Fair is fair, right? And when you distract me, you must be punished."

He played along with her teasing before kissing her lips quickly. He then released her, stating, "Okay, *ma shearc*, ye should pro'ly dry yerself and then off to bed with ye. I'll join ye when I'm finished with me bath." She allowed him to steady her as she stood, climbing out of the bathtub.

Maggie obeyed. After setting her alarm, she was sound asleep almost as soon as her head touched the pillow.

Shannon was true to his word and joined Maggie at the conclusion of his bath. Lying naked, he pulled her close to him, holding her skin to skin in the cradle of his body.

As he lay next to her sleeping form, Shannon pondered all of the lovemaking he and Maggie had shared over the past couple of days. He softly caressed the skin that covered her exposed hip. She was breathtakingly beautiful to him, and he couldn't remember the last time he had so thoroughly taken pleasure in the body of a woman. Further, she matched his passion and his sex drive.

Siobhan, on the other hand, had never been very interested in sex unless she stood to gain from it.

With Maggie however, he felt that she enjoyed it just as much as he, if not more. The thought nearly caused another boner to blossom, but this time, he managed to keep it reigned in, wanting to avoid waking her, or becoming uncomfortably erect.

Thoughts of the delicious things they had been doing replayed in his head over and over. As she lay still in his arms, he couldn't help but study her sleeping form. Caressing her had her moving against him.

Maggie muttered quietly in her sleep. At one point, he could've swore he heard her whisper "I love you Shannon". The thought alone brought tears to his eyes. There was just no way a woman as beautiful and good as Maggie could ever love him. And certainly not after so short a time. Siobhan had proven that to be true. She'd told him recently that women just couldn't love a man like him- he was too quick to laugh, *never takin' anathing serious*, she'd said. And that he was bloody lucky she ha' put up wit' the likes of him for all those years.

Shannon closed his eyes, attempting to shut out all of the horrible things he'd heard from his wife over the years. Unfortunately, this brought the wicked woman's wretched face straight to the forefront of his mind's eye. *Ghastly woman!* he thought.

Opening his eyes, he again studied Maggie. Her red hair was splayed out around her head like a halo, making her look like an ethereal angel. She had gone to bed without dressing, and he took the opportunity to really look at her, noticing the attributes she possessed that he had so thoroughly enjoyed before. Her breasts weren't very large; especially with her flat on her back. But he found he was quite fond of them. In fact, if given the choice between Maggie's perfect little perky tits, and Siobhan's very large and heavy ones, he'd have chosen the ones that currently lay next to him; the ones that fit so perfectly in his hands.

Staring at her breasts had him wanting to take her all over again. Unfortunately, she really did need to sleep, and he wasn't willing to start anything sexual while she was unconscious. In truth, what he was doing at that moment- looking at her without her permission- might have been crossing the line. *Nah!* he thought. Not after she had been doing the same thing to him just a few hours earlier. He really didn't think she'd mind after all that.

Suddenly a thought entered his mind unbidden. *What am I going to do about me wife, and what am I goin' to do about this bonnie lass?* Shannon just couldn't imagine letting Maggie go. He loved her too much. As this thought popped into his mind, his heart began beating wildly, and it became clear to him: he actually loved this woman. He wondered how it had happened so fast. He wanted to deny it, but it was impossible. And there it was plain and clear: the stark and undeniable realization that he had, in fact, fallen in love with her. What he felt for her was so different than anything he had ever felt for Siobhan. That woman could drop off the face of the earth for all he cared. The thought was actually pleasing to him. But of course it would never happen.

Resigned finally to the fact that there was nothing he could do about his predicament on this night, he decided that he may as well cherish his time with Maggie. Draping his leg over hers, he pulled her more securely against him, enveloping her in his body.

Eventually he fell asleep, still holding her close.

Chapter Four

Dr. David Schambaugh had just begun his morning rounds when his boss summoned him into her office. Dr. Martha Peters, an attractive neurology Attending in her early fifties, didn't tolerate much from her small group of Fellows, though she had always been impressed by David. As he entered her office, she looked up at him from her stack of paperwork with an expression which would easily cause a lesser man to become weak in the knees. For David, it was a huge turn on, and he had to stifle the urge to flirt with her.

"Have a seat, Dr. Schambaugh," Dr. Peters directed, nodding toward a chair near her desk, and wasting no time on small talk. He sat in the proffered chair as she got right down to business. "I've received a sexual harassment complaint from one of the nurse's aides; a Jordan Smithson," she informed him, skimming a document in front of her. "She alleges that you have made several suggestive comments to her, including but not limited to using the work 'fuck' at extremely inappropriate times, causing her to feel uncomfortable."

Dr. Peters paused, observing David from across her desk, awaiting his response. He had anticipated this and with a slight smile, he pulled a folded piece of forged paper out of his lab coat pocket. He began calmly dismissing the CNA's accusations, and he was incredibly convincing. "I was afraid she might pull something like this," David told Dr. Peters, shaking his head, feigning embarrassment for Jordan.

He unfolded the paper and placed it gingerly on her desk, paying close attention to her expression. Dr. Peters picked it up and began to look it over. As she read, a look of disbelief washed over her, causing her eyebrows to nearly reach her hairline. When she finished reading, she looked at David again, as if she was awaiting an explanation from him. "I found it in my lab coat pocket this morning, and I've found several more like this in my locker," he elaborated. "I've been hesitant to say anything because, well, I felt sorry for the girl and I didn't want her to get in trouble over it."

Dr. Peters studied David intently over the rim of her glasses, considering his explanation. Finally, she spoke. "Dr. Schambaugh, I don't believe I need to tell you just how serious an accusation of sexual harassment is, especially between a physician and a subordinate." The intensity of her stare made him feel like prey being stalked by a predator. He was forced to repress his fury at being reprimanded by a woman. Silently, he again began to fantasize about destroying the little whore who claimed he had been sexually harassing her.

He could almost feel the beginning of an erection, and had to reign in his imagination as well as his red-hot temper. "I apologize, Dr. Peters," David told her with all the faux sincerity he could muster. "Going forward, if a similar situation arises, I assure you, I'll promptly bring it to your attention."

With a slight nod, Dr. Peters lectured, "Please see that you do. In the meantime, I recommend that you stay as far away from Ms. Smithson as possible." With a dismissive gesture, she let him know that the conversation was concluded, and David rose from his chair and turned to leave. "Close my door," she instructed, as he exited her office.

As David turned the corner, he was consumed by a smoldering rage and the wheels in his head continued to turn as he vowed to seek vengeance.

****

At the hospital, Morgan and Maggie met with Lucia's nurse, who educated them on the symptoms for which they needed to be on the lookout in the child. After what seemed like forever, they were finally allowed to leave. They treaded carefully through the parking lot to Jasmine's Range Rover, which Morgan had borrowed, as it was much safer to drive through the ice and snow.

Settling into the passenger seat, Maggie fastened her seat belt and breathed a sigh of relief at not having seen David. She wasn't sure what she was going to do about him, in light of her newfound feelings for Shannon. David and Maggie's date was still on for the upcoming weekend, and she wasn't yet sure how to broach the subject with David or Shannon. Additionally, her mother's funeral was to be held the next day. The idea of going on a date with the doctor had her biting her nails, and she wondered how Shannon would react.

"Were you nervous about the possibility of seeing your doctor friend?" Morgan asked quietly, looking over at Maggie. Her face turned red for a moment. "Yes, I was, actually," Maggie admitted. Morgan was quiet for a few moments, but then asked, "Are you disappointed that you didn't see him?"

Maggie considered the question before responding. "Actually, no. I was hoping I wouldn't run into him," she told Morgan. "You know, Shannon and I…" Maggie stopped herself, unsure of how to finish her statement. What she and Shannon had been doing was great and, in fact, more amazing and more satisfying than she had ever dreamed sex could be. Maggie didn't feel like she owed Shannon an explanation; after all, they weren't in a committed relationship by any means. Not to mention the fact that he was still married. But she loved the way he made her feel, as though he hungered for her, seemingly unable to get enough.

Morgan waited patiently, but when Maggie continued to struggle to find words to express herself, she answered for her.

"You really like him, don't you?" Maggie nodded slowly and confessed, "I really do; so much, in fact, that it scares me."

As their vehicle waited at a red light, Morgan watched the expressions chase across her friend's face. She reassured her, letting Maggie in on a little secret. "Just so you know, John says he's never seen Shannon like this. He thinks he's head over heels in love with you."

In light of her friend's statement, Maggie couldn't control the wide grin that began to light up her face. She had never been in love, but she was certain it must be what she was feeling. Seeing her friend's contagious smile, Morgan smiled along with her. "You really do like him!" Morgan exclaimed.

Morgan had to once again focus on the road, as the light changed to green, but Maggie agreed with her, adding, "I think…I think I'm in love, Morgan. I never thought it would happen to me. But there's just this incredible chemistry between us. When I'm with him, I just feel so…complete!"

Their conversation was interrupted by Lucia, who called out from the back seat. "I'm hungry. Can we stop and get something to eat?"

They rode the rest of the way in silence until after the drive thru, Morgan asked, "What about his wife? He's married, right?" Maggie swallowed hard and acknowledged, "He is. But I overheard him on the phone with her last night, and it sounded like he's not interested in her at all. He just kept telling her over and over that he didn't want to see her. It was pretty pathetic; I guess she refused to take 'no' for an answer. Then she put someone else on the phone to try and convince him. He was pissed by the time he hung up."

Morgan processed the information for a moment, and then supplied new information. "Yeah, John said something about her being a horrible cheater, but that Shannon refused to believe it until she came out and admitted it to him."

"That reminds me of something he said last night," Maggie suddenly recalled. "It was something like…I can't remember exactly how he put it, but it was something to the effect of her having been pregnant by someone other than him, and that she had gotten multiple abortions. He seemed really bitter about it, actually."

The women were quiet for a while, absorbing this new information. When Morgan made it to the turnpike, she visibly relaxed, the road was much clearer. By then a gentle snow began to fall. Finally, Morgan spoke. "He seems like a good guy. I mean, seeing the two of you interact, or at least what little I did see…" She hesitated before asking the next question, then summoned the courage and whispered, "Did y'all…um…get together again?"

Maggie's smile spoke volumes, but she provided more details, stating, "It was amazing, Morgan; better than I ever thought it could be. In fact, I've never finished before, except when I've done it myself. But with Shannon, it's been every time."

Maggie knew that Morgan completely understood what she was saying, and figured that she felt the same way about John. Morgan didn't volunteer this information however, and Maggie thought it was likely because she didn't want to steal her thunder. Instead, she said, "That's fantastic, Maggie!" with a sigh of relief. When her friend looked at her quizzically, Morgan elaborated. "I've been thinking lately that you needed some hot sex." When Maggie remained puzzled, Morgan continued. "You've always been with selfish pricks who left you unsatisfied, and you deserve better than that. I've been hoping you would get with someone who would treat you how you deserve to be treated and who you would enjoy."

Maggie smiled at her friend's sentiment and thought of how different sex with Shannon had been. None of her exes could hold a candle to him or the pleasure he gave her. Then her thoughts turned to the mediocre sex she had had with David. At the time, Maggie had thought it was good, but compared to Shannon, it was disappointing at best. David had barely even touched her, and when he did it was while he still wore his scrubs. Now that she had another experience to compare it to, she realized that the sex she had had with David wasn't satisfying at all. Maggie decided right then and there that she would cancel her date with David. She simply couldn't justify continuing to see him when she was so intrigued with her new lover.

When they pulled into the neighborhood, Maggie's heart was pounding and her palms were sweaty in anticipation of seeing Shannon. She knew she was being silly, but couldn't help it. When Morgan parked in the circle drive in front of the house, Maggie could see Shannon standing on the porch smoking a cigar. His face lit up when he saw her. Before she could open her door, he was there, helping her out, holding her by the elbow so that she didn't slip on the ice.

"I hoped ye'd come back here, Maggie," he smiled. "I wanted to see if ye'd have dinner with me tonight." Arm in arm they walked inside, followed by Morgan and Lucia. Shannon didn't relax his grip until they were inside, safely away from the treacherous black ice that had accumulated on the front porch. Immediately, he escorted her to the guest room they had slept in the night before.

When Morgan entered, John was waiting for her at the foot of the stairs, and gathered her into his arms before kissing her lips in a heated embrace.

Surprised by the PDA, Lucia exclaimed rudely, "Whoa! How do her tonsils taste?" Unaccustomed to seeing the woman she thought of as her second mom in such a passionate embrace, her discomfort manifested in the form of sarcasm.

The couple ignored her for a moment, but when they finished devouring each other, John turned to the teenager and held his hand out to shake hers. "You may not remember me from the hospital, but I'm John, Morgan's boyfriend." Lucia stared at his hand in awe for a moment before remembering herself, and then she shook it.

"Let's get you settled in right away so that you can make yourself comfortable," he told her, as he guided her toward the small room to the side of the grand entryway. Her cheeks were flushed, and Morgan felt sorry for her for a moment, having a profound understanding of how John's charm could have an effect on a girl.

She listened as John showed Lucia around the room and smiled to herself until she was interrupted by the buzzing of her phone in her pocket. The screen showed a number she didn't recognize. She answered it cheerily, thinking it to be a prospective customer. On the other end of the line was the detective for Lucia's case asking when would be a good time for him to interview her daughter?

"Can you tell me what this is regarding, detective?" He was silent for a moment before explaining, "I believe she spoke with the perp during a recent house party, and we're interviewing everyone that was anywhere near that party." Morgan silently recalled Lucia mentioning that the dead guy had been with them at the party.

Glancing down at her watch, Morgan noted that it was just after 1 p.m. After a quick calculation, she advised the detective that she would have to consult with her mother before she could give him an answer. After hanging up, Morgan contacted her mom and was disheartened to learn that her family's return home was going to be further delayed by worsening blizzard conditions throughout the Midwest. When Morgan pressed for an ETA, she was told it would be Thursday at the earliest. Luckily she recalled the text she had received earlier that morning: school had been cancelled for the day due to deteriorating road conditions. After speaking with each of her children and then her father, Morgan hung up and called the detective, notifying him of the delay.

She had finally gotten off of the phone only for it to ring once more. Seeing that it was Mack, she groaned and rolled her eyes before answering it. "You still alive, Morgan?" he asked irritably. The last time she'd seen him was after she'd killed her stalker, so she understood why he was concerned.

"Yeah, I'm fine, Mack," Morgan said apologetically. "I'm sorry I haven't checked in with you. I've just been so…preoccupied lately." She thought maybe he knew what had kept her so "preoccupied," because she could hear a smile in his voice as said, "Oh? That new boyfriend of yours been keeping you busy?"

She silently cursed Mack's keen senses before responding. "I suppose you can say that," then hurriedly changed the subject. "The office open today?" she asked. He chuckled at the abrupt change, well-aware that it was an attempt to avoid the topic.

"You know it's not," Mack told her. "I sent texts to all of you. So, are you stayin' with him, or is he stayin' with you?" he pressed, circling back to the previous discussion. She scoffed at his boldness and said in a teasingly saucy voice, "Wouldn't you like to know!" Her retort had him laughing, and he responded, "Touché, my little employee of the year! I'll let you get back to…" Mack cleared his throat before continuing. "…that hot date of yours that I'd give my left nut to meet." Morgan nearly choked, barely managing to say goodbye before hanging up.

After getting her business squared away, she ascended the grand staircase, looking for John so that she could spend some of the time about which Mack had so rudely inquired. As she entered the master suite, she was pleasantly surprised that the door to the bathroom was ajar, and she could hear the shower.

When she pushed the door open, she was welcomed by a dense cloud of fragrant steam. John noticed right away when Morgan entered, and stepped out of the shower to greet her. Before she had the chance to remove her clothing, he wrapped his arms around her and firmly pulled her up against his sopping wet body.

"Mmmmm," he breathed into her neck, "where have you been all my life? You were only gone for a short while, but I've missed you terribly." He whispered to her in his thickening accent as he grinded against her hip with his growing erection. Suddenly, he pulled her away from him and ripped her blouse open. Clamping his mouth on her, he suckled first one nipple, and then the other, drawing it into his mouth. She hugged his head to her breasts, hastily removing her pants.

When there were no more barriers between them, they moved, almost as one, into the shower. She barely managed to pull the opaque door shut before he entered her with a force that had her pressed up against the shower wall. With a heaving, sensual sigh, Morgan cried out, "Oh my God, John! Don't stop!" He complied with her heated demand, repeatedly pounding into her until they orgasmed simultaneously.

They stood together against the shower wall, breathing heavily, as the tiles held them up. Finally, John moved, breaking the spell. Morgan looked up at him as they gazed into each other's eyes until he reached over and turned the water off. "Well," she said with a cheeky grin, "that was good clean fun!" John couldn't help laughing at her play on words as he grabbed a towel for her.

****

As soon as Maggie arrived, she and Shannon went to her room where a cheery fire crackled in the fireplace. The curtains were still closed, giving the room a cozy, warm feeling. Once the door closed behind them, Shannon grabbed Maggie by the hips and pulled her close so that she could feel his stiff shaft poking into her bottom. She grinded into him and he responded by groping her breasts. He then whispered in her ear, "Ye feel how badly I want ye, *mo ghra*!" as he rubbed himself firmly against her.

Maggie abruptly spun around, capturing Shannon's mouth with hers as she wrapped her hand around his throbbing erection. He gave her better access by shedding his pants before helping her to do the same. Their shirts gone, Shannon could wait no longer. He had to have her…now. He carried Maggie over to the bed, placing her on it in such a way that she was splayed out for his inspection.

Shannon looked down at Maggie, briefly studying her face. Gripping himself, he rubbed vigorously up and down, giving her a naughty, sexy show and building suspense, making her anticipation grow, just as his shaft was growing. Finally, he moved toward her, hovering on his knees. She shifted her position on the bed to accept him more effectively.

Unfortunately, his movements were interrupted by a banging on the door. Shannon paused and yelled toward the door. "Go away!" He continued to move over Maggie, eager to devour her.

"It's me, mate…I wouldna think ter interrupt ye, but it's important." Shannon paused in his movements, but didn't respond. Finally, Patrick called through the door, "It's ye're wife, mate. She said she thinks she's lost the babby."

Shannon looked at Maggie's face, regret clearly visible in his eyes as he backed off of her and then off of the bed. Leaning down to pull on his trousers, he told her, "I should go and see what this is about. Probably its bollocks, but me friend wouldna interrupt me without havin' a good reason."

After crossing the room to the door, Shannon turned and took one last regret-filled look at Maggie before exiting the room and closing the door behind him. Maggie felt as though she had been robbed, the sense of loss great. Suddenly, the grief she had repressed for the past few days came to a head, and she began to weep uncontrollably. Curling into a fetal position, Maggie cried until the blissful emptiness of sleep overtook her.

Chapter Five

When Maggie awakened, the winter sky had begun to darken, and she slowly removed the comforter from herself. The fire had died down and the room had a slight chill to it. She stood, stretched, and then went to the bathroom and brushed her teeth. Afterward, she checked her phone for messages. She was conscious of the fact that she was stalling in an attempt to delay facing Shannon. However when she opened the text message, she was glad:

On behalf of Smith Brothers Funeral Home, it is with sorrowful regret that we will need to delay your mother's wake due to inclement weather. It has been rescheduled for Thursday at 1 p.m., at which time the Weather Center states any ice will be well-thawed, and streets safe for travel. Please advise loved ones and other guests of this change. Our sincerest apologies for the inconvenience.

Maggie breathed a heavy sigh, once again feeling the sadness wash over her. Though she wasn't looking forward to her mother's funeral, she felt that delaying the service would only serve to prolong her grief. She sat down on the edge of the bed for a moment to collect her thoughts.

Sitting quietly until the sun's light was nearly gone, the vibration of her phone buzzing in her hand startled her. She stared at it briefly until awareness dawned on her, and then read the text from David Schambaugh:

I hope you are doing well. Haven't been in touch because work has been killer busy. Was looking forward to seeing you Friday night for the gala, but due to weather it was postponed til next week. If you're free, I still want to take you.

Maggie studied the message, considering the situation she was in. She had slept with two men within the last week. One had been mediocre at best, and that was the good doctor. The prospect of a relationship with a doctor- a neurology Fellow at that – was definitely tantalizing. To be with someone who had accomplished great things in the medical field was alluring, to say the least.

Then Maggie pondered Shannon and the intense chemistry they shared. The mere thought of what all they had done together made her throb with excitement, nearly creaming her panties. She could feel herself falling hard for him, but there was still so much she didn't know about him. *What does he did for work, and what are his living arrangements?* she wondered. For all she knew, he could be living in the basement of his parents' house. The idea of being in a basement triggered an image of satin sheets, black walls, and of Shannon chaining her up as he did delicious things to her. Maggie blushed bright red at the thought and decided to leave the sanctuary of the room, procrastinating any need to make a decision.

As she stepped into the hallway, she could hear voices mingled together in cheery conversation. It was reminiscent of what she'd heard the day before, except that this time, there were also female voices, as well as the high-pitched sounds of children mixed in.

By the time Maggie made it downstairs to the kitchen, the din had swelled, and she stood on the threshold, taking in the inhabitants of the household, gathered in a loose circle around the kitchen's massive center island.

An elderly woman was preparing something in an oversized mixing bowl, covered to her elbows in a dusty, floury mixture. She spoke animatedly to the children, who giggled intermittently. Lucia observed them in mute fascination, although wearing a look of faux aloofness, as the matronly woman playfully touched the spoon to the noses of the small children in teasing admonishment.

The two women, one of which included her best friend, stood leaning against the counter across from the children, their heads close together in schoolgirl-esque secrecy. Maggie could hear their periodic giggling as their heads lifted and they slyly stole glances at the men.

The group of men, which included Patrick, John, and a seemingly unconscious Shannon, were at the end of the counter opposite the door inside which Maggie stood. The brothers seemed to be having an enthusiastic discussion in their native tongue about something which Maggie couldn't understand. It was occasionally punctuated with one or each of them smacking Shannon heartily on the back, followed by boisterous laughter. The latest volley of blows were accepted with grunts and oafs. As Shannon's head rolled miserably to the side and his eyes opened slightly, she could see that he was actually awake, albeit attempting to ignore their shenanigans.

As Maggie surveyed the scene, she was mesmerized by the camaraderie and intimate familiarity between everyone in the kitchen. The setting brought to her mind large, loving families enjoying extended holidays together, sometimes having to agree to disagree, but overall, in genuinely affectionate companionship. For a moment, the sight had Maggie thinking of her own loneliness; it had recently been only she and her mother, as her mother's health had increasingly deteriorated, and they had little extended family to speak of. She shook her head in an effort to clear her mind, certain that this fleeting sadness was an effect of her overwhelming grief.

Maggie's reverie abruptly ended when Morgan spotted her. "Maggie, you're awake! I'm so glad you've joined us!" she exclaimed, practically skipping toward Maggie, pulling her in for a wholehearted embrace.

As their arms relaxed, Maggie glanced in Shannon's direction and saw that his eyes roamed the room until they settled on her face. He then watched Maggie as she and her friend crossed the kitchen to where Morgan had been.

"I received the text from the funeral home," Morgan told her. "I've already made the phone calls about your mom's funeral, so you don't have to worry about anything." Maggie was touched. "You did that for me? Morgan, thank you so much!" She closed her eyes, exhaling a great sigh of relief. Maggie hadn't realized she had been holding her breath, but the news her friend shared with her lifted a great weight from her shoulders, and she felt a sense of peace settle over her.

However, the joyful din in the kitchen was interrupted by Shannon, who was suddenly very close to Maggie and Morgan, demanding, "Ye've a wake ta go to that ye didna see fit to tell me about? Why did ye think ye needed to lie to me?" He was practically yelling in Maggie's face until his friends grabbed him by the arms, forcefully pulling him away from the women. Maggie stood still, staring at him in muted shock, trying to grasp the chaotic, if somewhat violent scene that had suddenly erupted.

The silence was interrupted by Brunne quietly, yet quickly, ushering the children through the door opposite where the men were huddled around Shannon in an attempt to subdue his suddenly explosive temper. The toddlers were easily led away, but Lucia stealthily hung back in an attempt to watch the commotion. Her attempt was met by quiet clucks from Brunne, chiding Lucia for her resistance. The girl slowly and reluctantly followed the others out of the kitchen.

With the young and old tucked safely away, the brothers relaxed their grip on Shannon, who began pacing, his anger only having been temporarily tamed, with the consequence of it surfacing anew once his restraints were loosened. When his circuit brought him near the group of women once more, the brothers became coiled, like cobras ready to strike, should he again become aggressive.

Having regained a semblance of composure, Maggie held her head high and took a step in Shannon's direction until they were quite close to each other once again, nearly face to chest. She looked up at him, maintaining eye contact so that they were each staring daggers at the other.

The others watched with bated breath, unsure of whether to intervene and risk inciting violence, or allow the two lovers their space so that they might attempt to reconcile. It seemed an eternity as no one moved or breathed as the angry duo stared at one another in seething hostility.

Suddenly, Maggie's hand snaked out like a lightning bolt, slapping Shannon square on the face with a single loud clap that broke the dead silence in the room. Shannon seemed to be oddly prepared for this, however; before she could retract her hand from his reddened cheek, he grasped her wrist and held her palm to his face holding her eyes with his.

Then he asked her in a barely audible voice, that was scarcely a whisper, "Why did ye keep your mum's death from me, Maggie? Is it always this way with women ye fall in love with that they feel they must hide things from ye?"

Maggie tried to pull her hand away as tears welled in her eyes. Not guilty tears, because she felt she had done nothing wrong. In fact, she hadn't intended to keep the information from him. It wasn't as if it was a secret. She had simply been so preoccupied– with him- that she honestly hadn't thought of it.

Maggie's tears were from the sadness she saw when she looked into Shannon's eyes. There was a deep hurt there; one that she hadn't caused, but a hurt all the same. And in the split second it took for her to summarize the swirling storm of emotions she saw in him, her heart ached for him.

As Shannon watched her, his face grew angrier and he all but threw Maggie's hand from his cheek. With one last frigid glance at her, he turned on his heels and stalked toward the door that led to his improvised guest room.

He looked as though he would enter, but at the last minute when he reached the doorway, he reared back, punching the wall with a strength that seemed super-human, leaving a sizeable hole. His actions, though meant to be destructive and concise, caused him to recoil, with a resultant fall so that he landed on his butt. After sitting quietly for a moment, he began to collect himself, shaking his head.

A bit wobbly as he attempted to stand, Shannon muttered, "Why do they always cry when ye catch 'em in a fib? It's no fair, it's no. Aye, downright dirty." Although speaking to himself, he had clearly forgotten that there were others in the room witnessing the spectacle he had created. Shannon opened the door to the office and went inside, slamming the door behind him, leaving the others staring in stunned silence at the closed door.

After what seemed like an eternity, a collective sigh was breathed. Patrick's and John's eyes settled on Maggie's progressively reddening face. Morgan was massaging her friend's neck in an effort to soothe her, and Jasmine was standing against the kitchen sink, as if for comfort, her arms wrapped around her own waist.

Morgan was angry on her friend's behalf and said, as if thinking aloud, "Dirty indeed! If he knew her, he'd know she doesn't cry so easily. What an ass!" Her statement had begun with her muttering to herself, but the last part was spoken somewhat louder than she'd intended.

Where John had been watching Maggie before, his eyes jumped to his lover's face, and he said rather heatedly, "I imagine my old friend has had enough of being lied to by the woman he loves. It tears a man down after a bit." Morgan looked up at him, stunned at the way he had spoken to her, but noticed that it was Jasmine at whom he was actually glaring during the final part of his statement.

Obviously still annoyed by his tone and his message, Morgan stood up straight, taking a step toward him; as much in defense of her best friend as of her once-lover, and began to speak, when she was interrupted by Patrick.

Likely seeing that his beloved was so deeply affected by the drama, his heart went out to her, and he felt he had to disengage the angry words that were surely about to occur. He stepped between Morgan and John and spoke up, "That's enough, you lot. There's been enough of a disturbance here. How 'bout you two go discuss ye're issues in ye're room. I'm takin' me girl out to our room in the guest house, and you, lassie, look as though ye could use a stiff drink."

Morgan began to protest that she wanted to stay to comfort her best friend, which Mag anticipated, and cut her off, telling her, "He's right, Morgan. I need a drink; a big one, along with a few moments to myself. Go with him for a while." When she continued to balk, Maggie calmly told her, "You can come check on me in a bit, Morgan." Then, with a small smile, reassured her, "I'll be fine. I promise."

Morgan reluctantly agreed to go, after hugging her best friend and kissing her on the lips. "I'll be back down in a bit," she promised, as she walked out with John. Patrick embraced Jasmine and together, they left the kitchen, his arms around her waist, comforting her.

Maggie watched the couple go and, for the second time in a short while, felt a twinge of longing, considering the protective gesture she had just seen Patrick display toward his love. Mag shook her head, discouraged, once again concluding that she would probably never experience that type of love.

Not bitter, but resigned to an ultimate life of solitude, Maggie found a large glass from the cabinet and poured herself a generous amount of whiskey from an unopened bottle. Holding her breath against the sweet, bitter heat that was sure to follow, she upended the glass in several large slugs, and then settled against the counter, staring at nothing and thinking about everything.

When her eyes began to water from her persistently staring into space, she looked down at the whiskey bottle and helped herself to another glass. This time, she sipped it slowly, as she thought of her mother's life, and the funeral that was three days away. Her heart ached for the loss of the mother to whom she had grown so close over the years. In fact, aside from Morgan, her mother had been her closest friend, and now she was gone.

Maggie swallowed hard several times to hold the tears in, and took a deep breath. She decided she needed to think of other things to avoid uncontrollably dissolving into tears.

As she sipped her whiskey, she thought back to Shannon's earlier behavior, and was thankful that she hadn't canceled with David. Not that she was any more interested in him. After the mind-blowing orgasms she had experienced with Shannon, the mediocrity of sex with David simply would not be sufficient.

She remembered the comments Shannon had made about his wife, coupled with what his friend had said when he interrupted them. Between that and Shannon's general dishevelment when she had appeared in the kitchen, Maggie decided that he was likely in a state of shock at having been told that his wife was pregnant; that is, if she had read the clues correctly. At this, she finished her glass of whiskey.

Mindlessly reaching for the bottle after several moments, Maggie had the feeling that someone had beat her to it, snapping out of her reverie. She looked over and saw that Shannon was watching her. Taking in his stance, it appeared that he had probably been there for some time. Maintaining steadfast eye contact with her, Shannon poured her a glass, and then filled the one next to it, which hadn't been there before.

They watched each other intently, draining their glasses seemingly in unison, as if in a silent challenge, and then both set their empty glasses down roughly on the counter. As they continued to hold eye contact, Maggie was certain something in him changed. At first, there was a smoldering anger, making his brown eyes appear almost black. The darkness shifted, first to sadness, and then to a smoldering passion. Maggie tentatively stepped toward Shannon, and then cupped his cheek where she had struck him.

To her delight, his arms went around her waist, and then descended, so that he was groping her rear and pulling her into him. He awaited her reaction as if trying to gauge her receptiveness to him. When she leaned into him, he leaned down and took her mouth with his. She kissed him forcefully, returning his passion while her hands roamed his body, squeezing his shoulders, and then his pecs, before forcefully grasping his hips and pulling him into her.

Shannon had to release her mouth so that he could take in some air. After a few quick gasps, he looked down at Maggie and told her with a sultry whisper, "I need to get ye in me room, love." With that, he picked her up, cradled her in his arms, and carried her into the office.

Shannon walked to the couch and set Maggie down as he held her to him, on his knees in front of her. With his face remaining close to her inner thighs, he hungrily removed her jeans. Leaning forward while parting her legs, he captured her delicate skin between his lips. Her breath hissed out as he tasted her, and her hands fisted in his hair. She held him close to her while pumping her hips, putting her more firmly against his mouth, his hot, moist breath on her flesh.

Almost instantaneously, Shannon had Maggie worked into a frenzy, her head tossing from side to side in ecstasy. He coaxed several orgasms from her as he stoked the fire into a raging conflagration. When she cried out his name, he released her and then, grasping her hips, pulled her forward so that she was perched on the edge of the couch, exactly where he wanted to enter her.

Maggie watched him through partially-open eyes, the anticipation of his presence within her clear on her face. Shannon poised himself just at her warm, swollen entrance, awaiting her permission. When she opened her eyes and looked up at him with an expression of naked wanting on her face, it was the answer he needed, and he thrust into her, eliciting a loud moan from her that was audible throughout the lower floor of the house.

He took her then, rhythmically thrusting into her, with a passion previously unfelt in him. As they fixated on one another, each seemingly gazing into the other's soul, Shannon's heart swelled with emotions he could not encompass, nor define, and he felt he would never be able to get enough of her. As she climaxed, Maggie's legs wrapped tightly around him as if to hold him locked to her, which he could not abide. Pushing her legs down, he then ascended his hands to rest, grasping her thighs, in an attempt to gain purchase while he pistoned into her, wanting to be even more deeply inside of her.

She took what he gave, accommodating him blissfully, until he could no longer keep it in, and he orgasmed, spewing his seed into her with one last enraptured thrust. Still attempting to process the sensations and emotions he felt, he collapsed on top of her in a heap of sweaty breathlessness.

Entranced in their thrall as they were, neither noticed when Morgan peeked in at them, seeking assurance that the sounds she had heard were not ones that signified abuse for her friend. Smiling when she realized she had merely heard the result of their lovemaking, she quietly closed the door, heading back to the bedroom where she and John had been arguing.

Chapter Six

When Morgan entered the master suite, John was still pacing, looking at her in silent consternation. Despite his intimidating stance, to Morgan, his anger seemed to have greatly dissipated. He watched her as she closed the door behind her, a slight smile in his eyes, along with his lips. Morgan, although still hurt by the sting of his earlier words, had calmed considerably as a result of seeing her friend so happily held in the throes of passion.

However, she still felt that she and John needed to discuss what had taken place earlier. Instead of giving in to his charm immediately and going to him, she stood leaning against the door, watching him. They studied each other in silence for a moment, until he sat on the bed, facing her, and patted the spot next to him in an unspoken gesture for her to join him.

Slowly, Morgan crossed the room and sat on the bed next to John. He turned to her with a lopsided grin and said, "*Mo shearc*, please accept my humble apologies." She looked up at him, her arms still folded defensively across her chest, and asked, "For what?"

His smile widened as he wrapped his arms around her. "You are going to make me tell ye what a *caffler* I been, aren't ya?" Morgan had been studying his features and trying to maintain a straight face, but when John used his Irish words and his accent thickened, she could no longer hold it in, and a quick laugh escaped.

She tried to cover it up by quickly clapping her hand over her mouth, but she realized that she had lost the battle to stay angry with him. Finally giving in, Morgan smiled at him, but demanded, "Yes. Tell me what a…caffler you are, whatever that is," trying out the new word on her tongue.

Seeing his triumph, John smiled at her, pulling her to him so that she sat on his lap. Taking advantage of her lost resolve, he kissed her lips as his hands roamed her body. Very quickly, Morgan was breathing heavily, ready to surrender to his shameful antics.

Shortly thereafter, he picked her up and laid her on the bed. While standing over Morgan, John gazed into her eyes. "I could tell ye, but I'd rather show you how very sorry I am, cara." He lowered himself onto the bed and inched over to her. After he managed to undress her, he pushed her thighs apart, descending so that his face hovered over the delicate folds of her most intimate skin.

Looking up at her over the slight, sensual curves of belly and breast, he whispered, "I'm afraid I'm going to enjoy my punishment at least as much as you." He then devoured her, bringing his mouth to clamp on to her. His tongue lathed at her, swirling, and dipping inside her channel. She rode his mouth on a wave of pleasure until she was forced to grip his head in an attempt to hold on, and not be washed away by the havoc he was wreaking on her body.

When she was on the edge of climax, he increased the pressure on her nub, causing her to explode into his mouth. He knew she had orgasmed, but he continued his assault, waiting for her to beg him to enter her. Relentlessly, he continued until finally, she cried out, "John, please!" Her plea was nearly a whisper, perhaps more aptly described as a husky groan.

Immediately, he rose to his knees. In order to keep her head from banging against the headboard, he grabbed her by the hips and pulled her toward him in a violent tug as he entered her. John loved watching Morgan's face as he reignited the passion within her. Eyes closed, she quietly moaned, willingly taking everything he gave her, until he heard his own voice cry out, and with a last frantic push, his release was achieved, his seed pouring into her. He gradually lowered himself down, so that he rested over her.

Rubbing her cheek tenderly, John looked passionately into her eyes. "Morgan, I love you."

She caressed his cheek and then shifted her position to accommodate his weight more comfortably. While looking in his eyes, she returned his affection, stating, "And I, you, John... These last several days have been...heaven on earth for me." She opened her mouth and then closed it. It seemed she didn't know exactly what she wanted to say; she just appeared overwhelmed from the emotions that coalesced just beneath the surface.

John spared her the need to elaborate, telling her, "That's exactly how you make me feel, love. I am speechless in your presence, and the love I feel for you...I must say thank you, Morgan. You have given me so much."

Morgan was clearly touched by his exaltation, appearing to be close to tears. Smiling in response, it seemed she felt the same way. As she snuggled into his chest, she told him, "Ditto doesn't seem to say it well enough, John, but I feel exactly the same way about you."

John's arms enveloped her as they moved closer together. He then wrapped his legs around hers, sheltering her in his body. Leaning down, he kissed the top of her head, and then asked, "Morgan, what does that word mean...ditto?"

His query elicited a short burst of laughter. When he looked at her askant, she explained teasingly, "Well-traveled, well-cultured man that you are, you don't know the word 'ditto'?" John feigned offense for a moment, huffing dramatically, until she pinched his nipple. In retaliation, he pinched her bottom, causing her to squeal loudly.

"Well!" Morgan told him, after a bit. "Whatever you pinch, you must soothe, Mr. Kennedy," she ordered, using her best school marm's voice. John smiled and, grabbing her forcefully by the hips, sat her bottom on his face, while he proceeded to lick and kiss the reddened skin. After thoroughly relieving any irritation, he picked her up just as he had before, replacing her so that she was wrapped in a tangle of his arms and legs. "Now it's your turn, lover," he playfully reminded her.

So caught up in his ministrations, Morgan had neglected to care for his offended nipple. After a moment of her staring blankly at him, he gestured to the teat in question. She licked her lips as she looked down at it, and then brought her mouth to it. Seductively sticking out her tongue before she arrived at her destination had him making a low, almost growling noise in his throat, and she smiled, likely finding joy in the knowledge that she could make him as crazy as he made her.

Capturing it between her lips, she swirled her tongue, softly at first, before sucking it into her mouth. Nibbling it lightly had him moaning, while his hand made its way to his phallus, where it began a slow, firm massage.

Making an effort to take more of him in her mouth, she gently flicked the head in between thrusts, and then looked up at him with wide eyes, awaiting his direction. Enjoying their game, John would not disappoint. Very quickly, he teasingly scolded her. "Now look at what you have done, naughty girl." He flicked his shaft toward her, causing a pearly white drop to dislodge, and land in his curly hairs.

Continuing his mock admonishment, he groused, "You have caused Willie to cry with your abuse. You must kiss him and show him you still love him." Morgan giggled at the fake voice he used, but then went to work, swirling her tongue over him, from tip to scrotum.

As she set herself to work on her task, low guttural moans escaped his throat, and he fisted his hands in her hair, encouraging her to take him deeper and harder. While John had studied Morgan, noting her sexual preferences, Morgan had obviously done the same for him, as she seemed to note his. Very quickly, she built the pleasure for him until, although he tried to hold out, he could not. With a loud grunt, he buried his hands against her scalp, and with one last tense thrust, emptied himself down her throat.

With obvious pleasure, Morgan lifted herself on her elbows, smiling up at him. She then took her place at his side, snuggling into the warmth of his body. When he had finally composed himself somewhat, John persisted, "You still did not answer my question, Morgan. What does 'ditto' mean?"

She caressed his cheek, answering, "I'd rather show you than tell you. But first, have you ever seen the movie, *Ghost*?" Morgan seemed to already know the answer, but John's brief head shake was the confirmation she needed. Retrieving her phone from the bedside table, she went to work accessing her iTunes account. Settling into a comfortable position next to her lover, she started the movie for him. Her slyly stolen peeks told him she was curious to see whether he liked it.

****

When Patrick closed the door behind him, he could feel Jasmine trembling in his arms, no doubt shaken up from the events that had taken place in the kitchen. When he sensed that she would walk away from him to hide herself in the bathroom, he tightened his grip, pulling her into him. She turned her face away from him, appearing embarrassed by what her husband had said.

Patrick didn't let her move away from him. Determined to see her through her miasma of emotions, he lightly grasped her chin and lifted it up. He needed to look into her eyes; needed her to look into his soul, and glean from him that he accepted her...all of her, unconditionally. "Listen to me, *mo shearc*," he said quietly, as he leaned down to kiss her neck. Though he knew she wanted to resist him, his lips caressing her skin had her moving into him.

When he recognized that he had her attention, Patrick pulled Jasmine closer to him and walked toward the bedroom, prompting her to accompany him. His erection pressed into her, and eventually her frown was replaced by a smile, as he settled her onto the bed. He looked down at her, whispering, "Listen, *a ghra mo chroi*, me heart's beloved," he translated for her. "Me brother is angry still, and he speaks out of anger. But it is no matter. You are my beloved, and I know with every fiber of my being that ye were meant for me."

He caressed her face gently, and then kissed her softly before continuing. "In time he will get over it. That is, when he sees tha' we were meant to be together. You were made for me, and we fit. He never would ha' been happy havin' ya, nor you him." As Patrick spoke these words, he stared into her eyes, pleading with her to understand.

Finally, Jasmine smiled and brought her face to his. After a passionate kiss, she exclaimed, "Patrick, I don't know what I would do without you, or what I've done to deserve you, but thank you!"

He kissed her again, unable to keep his lips from her. When his kisses descended to her breast, she held him there for a moment, her hips thrusting into him. Soon, he could control his excitement no longer, as she embraced him more firmly, her legs tightening around his waist.

"Aye, I want ye too," he expressed, as he held her to him. He couldn't help that he had lengthened, so that his shaft pressed into her…his damn cock seemed to have a mind of its own. He was wanting to comfort her, but he had to contend with the intrusion of his growing, ignorant phallus. But Jasmine didn't seem to mind, as she eagerly wriggled out of her jeans. Before he knew it, Jasmine had them both stripped from the waist down, and was pulling Patrick on top of her.

"How do ye want me, love?" he asked, as he gazed down at her face. Before answering, she raised up and kissed his lips, stabbing her tongue deep, exploring his mouth. When she finally lay back, breathless, she answered in a husky voice. "Slow, the way you do it, Patchy. It's my favorite at times like this."

He obeyed, taking her slowly, and drawing out the pleasure for both of them. Languorously, he rode her, stretching her deliciously, enjoying the intimate world that the two of them created together. He watched the expressions chase across her face with each thrust. Her silent moans told him everything he needed to know: she was thoroughly enjoying the way he made love to her.

Patrick was so turned on by his lover that his climax was very close. Merely looking at her made him want to cum, but he couldn't do that to her; she needed to orgasm first, lest he deflate, leaving her unsatisfied. Closing his eyes to her beauty, he pictured the old woman he had seen on the news that morning, allowing him to experience only the sensations where he and his lover joined.

Suddenly, he felt Jasmine's hands gripping his arms. Her body lifted frantically to meet his for several rotations. As he opened his eyes, her face was so beautiful to him. He loved watching her as she orgasmed; her expression was so peaceful and conveyed such deep loved. Just then, he could hold back no longer, and spewed into her, gloriously spending his own orgasm. Unable to hold himself up any longer, he collapsed on top of her.

When the pleasured convulsion finished, he lay next to her, studying her drowsy face. While he reigned kisses on her, Jasmine opened her eyes as if suddenly remembering a task needing to be done. She looked Patrick directly in the eyes. "I forgot to mention it earlier, but your appointment…" She trailed off hesitantly, the pause allowing him to process the change of topic. "They can get you in on Friday at 3pm."

Patrick settled onto his back, head resting on his forearms, as the wheels in his head began to turn. He had conflicting emotions about the upcoming visit. On one hand, if what Jasmine told him was true, it could be that he had what she'd called "brain fits." If that turned out to be the case, while it would be a tremendous relief, it would also mean he had an ailment of some kind.

On the other hand, if he was found to be of sound mind, what would that indicate? Would it prove Breanna's accusation all those years ago to be true; that he was, in fact, a rapist? And if so, what would that do to his relationship with Jasmine? He couldn't bear the thought of hurting her or putting her through any more anguish than she had already endured.

In all honesty, Patrick was at an impasse that was dependent upon the outcome of this upcoming appointment, a mere four days away. If the result was that he was deemed a rapist, plain and simple, he would be faced with a difficult decision. He knew that it would more than likely be the most difficult of his life: leave Jasmine in order to avoid harming her, yet hurt her with his absence…or remain with her and face the very real possibility of wounding her in the worst way imaginable.

Patrick closed his eyes tightly against the thought of the decision he would soon potentially face. He felt a lump begin to well up in his throat as he imagined Friday's possible outcome. Remembering that his love was next to him, he swallowed several times to prevent the tears that threated to fall. At all costs, he wanted to protect Jasmine from himself…including from his tears.

When he opened his eyes, Jasmine was staring down at him as if studying his face for a hint of insight into what he was feeling. Patrick started to speak, to comfort her, but something in her expression stopped him. She laid her arm lightly on his chest, proclaiming, "We can face anything together, Patrick." She searched his eyes for a moment, moved her face close to his, and reassured him. "You are safe with me, my beloved."

He listened, captivated by her openness, and by the depth of the unconditional love she was offering. The emotions bubbled up, and he couldn't hold back the single tear that slid down his cheek. She captured it, and then pulled him to her, so that he was cradled to her breast.

"I love you, Patrick. Together we can face anything. And I don't give up so easily on the ones I love." He remained snuggled into her bosom, secure in the nurturing peace that had evaded him for so long. Eventually they slept, Patrick cocooned peacefully in her loving embrace.

****

As Jordan Smithson left a long, hard day of turning patients, taking vital signs, and cleaning feces from patients' reddened bottoms, she couldn't help but smile. Her "work wife," as she had begun to think of Samantha, the other CNA that worked with her, always had her laughing hysterically at her outrageous antics.

Jordan considered their friendship for a moment, deciding that she liked where they had arrived. Though not always friendly, ever since their one tryst following the boss's Christmas party, they had gotten on quite well. Reflecting further on their past, Jordan recalled that when she had first started working on the unit as a tech, Sam had been something of a bully, calling her out for simple mistakes and making her feel quite incompetent.

However, after the Christmas party at Miss Joan's house at which Jordan had become highly intoxicated, things had changed. Though the details were foggy, Jordan remembered bit and pieces; she had become involved in a highly intimate, erotically-charged situation, finding herself wearing only her birthday suit in Sam's bed. After fully awakening, the two had then become fast friends. Thinking back, however, Jordan had a nagging feeling that when she and Sam were naked, passionately kissing, vagina to vagina and breast to breast, that there were things about that night she did not quite remember accurately…though Sam had assured her that nothing more had taken place beyond the kissing that Jordan had discussed with her.

Mentally shaking these unsettling feelings, Jordan walked the last few feet to her car and inserted her key to unlock the door. She heard a muffled sound from somewhere close to her car, and half-heartedly looked in the sound's direction. Dismissing it as paranoia, she hurriedly opened the driver's door, settling into the driver's seat of the classic VW bug. After starting the engine, she glanced into at her rearview mirror, preparing to back out of her parking space. Suddenly her heart jumped into her throat: from the back seat, Dr. Schambaugh's eyes stared back at her in the mirror.

Quickly spinning in her seat to look at him, she slapped his chest, exclaiming, "Dr. Schambaugh! What on earth are you doing here?" The hit was harder than she had intended, but was a knee-jerk reaction she couldn't help.

The two sat watching each other as observations endlessly fired into Jordan's consciousness. The doctor was crouched in the middle of the back seat. His expression was calculated and cunning; lethally calm, and reminiscent of a deadly predator. His teeth were barred, visible around the snarl of his tight lips. A reflective glint caught Jordan's eye, and subconsciously the thought glimmered that it was a knife tucked into the waistband of his scrubs. Something in the back of Jordan's mind screamed at her, supplanting the sudden urge to run away from this man. She urgently needed to get out of her car.

Gritting her teeth, she mentally pushed down the emotions, as she had taught herself to do in situations like this. *You're just being silly*, she told herself. *He's a doctor; he would never hurt you…you don't want to look crazy in front of this hottie. Everyone would laugh at you if they knew what you were thinking.* As she frantically worked to convince herself that she was safe, she forced herself to release her death grip on her seat and relax. *Just smile and be nice until he leaves,* she convinced herself.

David watched the girl in front of him as she stupidly and naively stared at him. With efficient precision he evaluated her reaction. Swiftly taking in details, he calculated her response as well as her thought processes. He could see terror in her eyes which served to amp up his sexual excitement. As he studied her, he knew that she was fighting her base instinct to run. Ready to grab for his knife should there be need, his grip tightened momentarily on the hilt. Her gaze flickered to his hand before she took a deep breath and appeared to force herself to relax.

When David continued to remain silent, Jordan laughed nervously. "Dr. Schambaugh, how did you know this was my car? If you wanted to see me again, all you had to do was ask," she told him, watching his features, in a feeble attempt to justify his presence.

With her provided ammunition, David smiled charmingly at her, feigning surprise. "Oh, is this your car? I can't imagine how I ended up here." When Jordan laughed weakly again he suggested, "In any case, how 'bout you and me go for a pleasant afternoon jaunt?"

Sensing her hesitation, he convincingly assured, "I will be a perfect gentleman, I promise. I just want to get to know you away from work a little better." He could see by her expression that she was unsure of what to do.

Smiling at her again, he leaned forward, shackling her arm and effectively barring any escape. In order to ease her into her newfound captivity, he kissed her on the mouth, biting her lip. "That's more like it, pet," he stated, displaying the expression that served him so well in these situations. The way she sunk into the seat told him what he needed to know: he had her submission. Retaining his hold on her arm, he settled more comfortably in the back seat, studying her. He could literally see the hair on her neck standing on end. Jordan, obviously resigned to her fate, smiled nervously and complied. "Okay, doctor, where shall I take us?"

This time, David's smile was genuine, although he knew, much more sinister. He was relieved that she was no longer turning to look at him. Instead, she was looking in her rearview mirror as she backed out of her parking spot. "Oh, not far from here," he said casually, preparing to direct her to his apartment.

Chapter Seven

On Tuesday, Oklahoma City was still blanketed with inches of ice that effectively shut down all but the bravest of travelers. Naturally, the two young girls were anxious to play in the snow.

"Come on, Mama," whined Callie, "Let's go build snow man." Jasmine couldn't help but smile at her baby. She had always adored the enthusiasm and endless energy of young children. Before she could speak, Patrick piped up. "Ye want to go sledding, me lil' lass?" he asked Callie, scooping her up before tickling her relentlessly.

The small child's delighted squeals echoed throughout the house, catching the attention of her older sister. "If she gets to go, I want to go too," Deirdre demanded crossly. Usually a contrary child, her disposition became even sourer at the prospect of her younger sister getting the opportunity to enjoy an activity while she didn't.

Watching Patrick with his child-or so she thought-Jasmine smiled. He had always been naturally good with children. But as he held the toddler, twirling her around as she giggled, and carrying her around the room, she could see the pride gleaming in his eyes. Further, his joy seemed to match Callie's, as he played his game, raising her high overhead, imitating an airplane.

As Deirdre stood, solemnly taking in the fun, she began pouting, arms folded across her chest. Jasmine noticed the differences in each girl's personality. Where Deirdre was such a serious, thoughtful child, Callie found unabashed delight in even the smallest things.

Jasmine's observations were interrupted when John walked into the kitchen. Seeing him, Deirdre's somber face suddenly lit up and she ran to him, throwing herself into his arms. John caught her as he watched his younger brother with her little sister. "Daddy, will you make me be an airplane too?" Deidre pleaded. Unwilling to be outdone by Patrick, John complied, lifting her high into the air and soaring her around the kitchen.

Before long, the kitchen had grown quite noisy with the squeals and laughter of the two young girls, imitating birds and airplanes. The racket did not go unnoticed by other occupants of the household who began filing into the room to see the source of all the commotion. "Well, who's gonna twirl *me* around?" Lucia quipped, to the laughter of Morgan, just entering.

Finally, the two men, worn out from the strain of carrying wriggling little bodies over their heads, put the girls down.

"Well?" Deirdre asked, hands on her hips, looking expectantly at Patrick. He turned to Jasmine and solicited her input. "What do ye think? Can we go sledding, love?"

Jasmine readily conceded. "Yes. I think a field trip so that we can get the girls out of the house is definitely in order." This elicited excited giggles from both girls, and muted laughter from Lucia.

"Remember to dress warmly," Morgan reminded, disappearing into the hallway. "You just got better; I don't want you to get sick again."

Over her shoulder, Lucia assured, "I will, Morgan. You don't have to worry about me."

Patrick and Jasmine took the girls upstairs to prepare them for the frigid outdoor weather, leaving Morgan and John alone in the kitchen. John took the opportunity to wrap his arms around her and pull her close for an intimate embrace. The two inhaled each other while kissing.

The rest of the day passed uneventfully, with Shannon and Maggie hibernating in her room for the day, and John and Morgan snuggling in his bed, watching movies. Morgan was pleased to learn that he actually enjoyed many of the classics she loved.

****

Jordan awakened in her apartment, disoriented, and with the worst headache she had ever had in her life. She slowly managed to sit up, immediately regretting it. With little warning to find an appropriate receptacle or reach the bathroom, her stomach seemed to explode, its contents forcefully exiting her body, painting the comforter a sickening green.

She heaved for what seemed like hours, thinking that surely, with nothing remaining in her stomach, the violent retching could not continue. When it finally subsided, she settled herself on the pillows in an attempt to get comfortable, wiping her sweat-slickened forehead with the back of her hand.

When she was finally able to draw a deep breath, Jordan gradually began to notice the sensations in her body. To her shock, she realized she was completely naked. With a worsening headache, she strained to remember what had taken place the night before. Struggling to see through the fog that seemed to blur the time in question, she pushed the cover back.

Examining the areas of her body that she was able to see, she discovered with horror that her breasts were tender and noticed that the tips were reddened. The pale, supple skin was covered with angry bruises. As she continued assessing her body, she saw that her inner thighs were also bruised, but in a pattern that appeared suspiciously like finger marks.

Jordan became increasingly disturbed when the thought occurred to her that the various marks on her body were consistent with rough sex-or worse-forceful, violent sex. Gently placing one hand between her legs, she felt an intense sting. This, coupled with the blood on her fingertips, had her mind reeling and grasping desperately for a plausible explanation.

Her head began to spin, making it even more difficult to recall the events of the previous evening. She closed her eyes, hoping that less stimuli would help her concentration. Unfortunately, as hard as she tried, she was unable to recollect her last memory.

Opening her eyes, Jordan looked around her bedroom in an attempt to jog her memory. Seeing her scrub top draped over her dresser revealed that she had been at work the day before; yet she couldn't remember leaving work. Closing her eyes once again, she pictured her friend Sam, and was then able to remember having eaten lunch with her in the crowded break room.

Jordan became dizzy, alarmed, and frightened by the void that had been the last several hours. Taking a deep breath, she struggled to remain calm. She slowly inched herself toward the edge of the bed, where she managed to stand and take a tentative step, testing her proprioception.

Realizing that she was able to stand, she stepped away from the bed, wrapping the sheet around her, and went looking for her phone. As if telepathically sensing her need, at that moment it began ringing. She could tell the sound was coming from the living room. Gradually, she made her way toward the ringing and picked up the phone. To her horror, she discovered that it was five in the evening, meaning she had overslept and was late for her evening shift.

Looking at the phone, she could see that Sam was calling; no surprise there. Before Jordan could speak, Sam frantically asked, "Oh my gosh, girl; are you okay?" Suddenly, she wanted to cry. Partly because she wasn't sure if she was, in fact, okay; and partly due to the unsettling feeling that she was losing her mind.

She opened her mouth to reassure Sam, and…silence. Nothing came out. She was unable to speak, and couldn't form coherent words. When Jordan finally managed to force sound from her throat, it came out in a moan that quickly morphed into a sob. To her dismay, it seemed that once the dam had broken, there was no controlling the forlorn wailing from escaping from deep within.

Fortunately, Sam immediately realized that there was something terribly wrong. "Stay right there, Jordan. I'm on my way," she ordered. Jordan ended the call and did the only thing she felt she could do, which was curl up into a fetal position and cry. Numbly, she wondered if her crying was from what she was sure had happened to her, or from what she couldn't remember happening. Closing her eyes to the onslaught of emotions, she decided it didn't really matter why she was crying, and awaited the arrival of her friend.

****

While waiting for Sam, Jordan drifted back to sleep from the combination of emotional exhaustion along with the aftereffects of whatever had happened to her the night before. Therefore, she didn't hear Sam ring the doorbell or her insistent knocks on the door until it became a heavy banging. After rousing enough to stand, Jordan shuffled unsteadily to the door and let her friend inside.

Seeing a familiar face elicited another cascade of tears, and Sam held Jordan in her arms, comforting her as she fell apart. When Jordan managed to stem the flow of tears and resume a semblance of her normal breathing pattern, Sam looked into her eyes, assuring, "I've got you. I'm here." She gently brushed the hair out of Jordan's face and instantaneously noticed the vicious marks on her neck that extended down the front and further down, beyond the top of the bedsheet which was wrapped around her.

Looking up from where she had been resting her head on Sam's shoulder, Jordan sniffled and sheepishly admitted, "I don't know what's wrong with me, Sam. I'm not sure what happened, or even if anything *did* happen."

Sam caressed her cheek. "Shh…shh," she whispered. "The medics are on their way, baby doll. If nothing else, they can check you over and try to find the missing pieces." As if the mere mention of them summoned their arrival, a paramedic appeared in the doorway, to Jordan's dismay. Seeing the look of alarm on her friend's face, Sam quickly explained, "I couldn't get you to answer the door. I was worried about you." She then awkwardly admitted, "The police had to be called also," as she avoided her friend's gaze.

Before there could be any further discussion, the paramedics ushered Jordan onto the stretcher and began working on her. As she was assisted to lie down, the sheet was inadvertently pushed up above her knees, and Sam spotted the finger-shaped bruises and dried blood in stark contrast to her pale skin. Jordan sat in stunned silence, remaining thus until a police officer appeared in her doorway.

Seeing that Jordan was alert, the officer's expression quickly changed from one of concern to irritation. "So, I take it there's no need for police assistance then?" he assumed, pivoting, with one foot already out the front door.

"Hold up a minute!" Sam called out, in an effort to put a stop to his abrupt departure. He paused and partially turned so that his body was mostly outside of the apartment, but did not re-enter.

Looking at Sam with obvious annoyance, he muttered, "Eh?" as if she had told him that she liked to dance naked on the moon.

"Something has happened to her, officer. It's apparent just by looking at her, and I think a police report needs to be filed." His arms came up to cross over his chest, resting atop his robust, cauldron-shaped abdomen. He looked at her in silence for a few moments, almost as if he hoped his glare could make Sam retract her statement, but to no avail.

Finally, he turned to look at Jordan and studied her face, as if silently willing her to disagree with her friend. His glare went unnoticed, however, as she remained in a stunned daze. Seeing that he was getting nowhere, the officer turned to Sam in irritation. "What is this? The girl isn't even talkin', let alone askin' to file a report, and I can't do nothin' without her talkin' to me." As if his observation settled it, he turned from the scene in the crowded apartment and disappeared.

Sam was more than slightly vexed at his behavior and attitude, but she persisted in her demand for the necessary care for Jordan. Turning to the medics, she pulled an unoccupied one away from the stretcher and quietly insisted, "Look, she needs a forensic exam; I don't care *what* that fat bastard said."

The attendant, more sympathetic to the patient's plight, nodded and assured Sam that he would ensure that it happened. Stepping into the bedroom, he placed a phone call, leaving Sam to watch over Jordan, who was still staring blankly into space.

Shortly thereafter, the medic returned and informed the others that they would be transporting Jordan to Baptist Medical Center for evaluation. Basic assessment completed, Jordan was wheeled into the apartment's breezeway, and in short order loaded into the awaiting ambulance.

Once the rear door was closed, the sympathetic medic told Sam, "It was my boss that I called. Sexual assault exams are being conducted at Baptist this month. You should probably drive there; they can take some time, and she may need a ride home afterward."

Sam nodded in agreement and walked to her car, after peering through the ambulance's rear door window at a still-stunned Jordan.

In silence, Sam followed the ambulance, not even listening to music for fear it would distract her. Her mind's eye wouldn't stop replaying the telltale injuries she saw on her friend. She felt so numb and stricken by the anger and fear she felt for Jordan that it seemed to constrict her chest, making it difficult to suck in a full breath.

The drive to the hospital felt like an eternity, though in actuality, it was less than ten minutes. When they finally arrived, Sam whipped into a parking space as the ambulance pulled into its designated entry point at the rear of the emergency department. Deciding to take the more expedient route into the building, she approached the ambulance as Jordan was being wheeled out of it, and then fell into place, blending in with the entourage. They were taken directly to a room where Sam sat quietly with her friend to await medical care.

After nearly an hour of sitting alone together in total silence, Sam was startled when Jordan suddenly remarked, "They brought me here because they think maybe I was..." She trailed off, unable to finish verbalizing the conclusion she had drawn, but looked to her friend, as though for guidance.

"Raped," she finished for her, with a finality to her tone that left no room for question as to what had happened to her. Before either could speak, a woman in a long white lab coat entered the room. "Hi Jordan. I'm Annie, and I'm the nurse practitioner who's going to take care of you for part of this visit. Is it okay if I ask you a few questions before we get started?"

Jordan stared dumbly at her for a moment before nodding, giving the NP the opportunity to begin. "All right. First, let me ask you: what was the last thing you remember before waking up and deciding to come in for a SANE exam?"

Sam spoke up for her friend, defiantly opposing the query. "My friend's mind is just fine," she exclaimed, heatedly. After standing up and taking a step toward the lady, she continued, "She's quite sane, so that's not the issue here. She needs a forensic exam."

To the surprise of both Sam and Jordan, the thin line of Annie's lips along with the furrow in her brow lifted, and she gently explained, "I apologize for the confusion, ladies. The SANE exam has nothing to do with your mental faculties. SANE is just an acronym for sexual assault nurse exam, and as such, there is a specially trained nurse on the way to conduct yours. I'm just here to do your medical clearance; to make sure that you are physically stable."

The room was quiet as the two women absorbed this information. Suddenly, Jordan piped up. "Sexual assault? But I don't even *know* if anything happened; I'm not even sure of where I was last night. Surely..." she trailed off, unsure of how to articulate her thoughts.

The room remained silent as she attempted to put her thoughts in order. Finally, she sputtered, "I don't know if I can do this. I can't even remember anything past lunch yesterday."

Annie briefly contemplated Jordan's concerns before formulating her response. She swallowed visibly and softly suggested, "Perhaps you would consider having the exam done.

Many times, there is no clear picture of preceding events, but a forensic exam can help to explain…things."

Jordan thought this over. Having difficulty processing it, she looked to Sam for direction. "Sexual…assault?" Jordan finally asked, as if actually speaking the words aloud would help her reach some logical conclusion. She grasped at straws but nothing came to her, as the two other women in the room awaited Jordan's decision.

Annie and Sam sat patiently, anticipating instructions from the patient in the bed, as the silence stretched. Finally, Jordan mumbled, "I don't know. I need to think about it for a minute." Annie nodded, then stood and walked toward the door. Pausing, she gave a quick look at Jordan before stepping out, closing the door behind her.

Seeing that Sam was still seated, Jordan added, "Alone, Sam. I need a minute alone, please." Sam was somewhat taken aback, but nodded in understanding, rose from her chair, opened the door, and stepped out of the room.

Jordan turned toward the phone at the side of the bed and dialed the only person she could think of who might possibly offer some valuable input. When the call was answered, she said, "Auntie Serena?" in order to verify the identity on the other line before continuing.

To Jordan's relief, it was her aunt that picked up, and she recounted for her in detail the dire circumstances in which she had found herself. Her aunt listened, only speaking up to ask the occasional question.

When Jordan had finished explaining the situation, her aunt's reaction stunned her.

"So, let me get this straight. You expect me to believe that you remember nothing from yesterday, and now you're saying that your dike friend thinks someone took advantage of you, girlie?" The suspicion and anger in her aunt's voice cut Jordan to her very core, and she felt an ache there as the tirade continued. "Jordan, if I've told you once, I've told you a thousand times. You've got to learn to tell the truth, girl! Just like what you said about your stepdaddy that got me stuck with you. Men ain't tryin' to touch you against your will every time you turn around. You just need to face facts and admit you want sex all the time, girl!" Jordan couldn't bear to hear anymore. She slowly opened the hand which held the phone and allowed it to fall to the floor.

Upon hearing the clatter, Sam entered the room. She noticed how pale Jordan's face had become. Sam caught her breath and guessed, "What happened? Did you remember last night?"

Jordan couldn't make herself answer, as her tongue was stuck to the roof of her mouth. As she sat in shock, numbly trying to process her aunt's horrible accusations, she closed her eyes, wanting nothing more than to descend into a deep sleep and hibernate forever.

After several minutes, Jordan opened her eyes to see a new person in the room. Before she could ask, Sam introduced her. "This is Jenna from the rape crisis center. She's a sexual assault advocate, and I thought you might like to hear what she has to say."

In a daze, she closed her eyes. While she heard the advocate speaking, she wasn't listening particularly closely. The advocate's voice almost seemed distant at times, as if it was coming from another room. Jordan only managed to catch a phrase here and there: "It's about power and control....not your fault....walk down the street naked, no one has the right to have sex with you."

It was difficult for Jordan to process the information that Jenna, the advocate, was trying to impart, although she could sense the genuine compassion in her voice. She felt like she had the time she witnessed a fatal automobile accident: unable to process reality, feeling separate from her body, and muted in disbelief. Mostly, she sat still in the bed, only opening her eyes at brief intervals to note whether there had been any new arrivals to her own personal hell.

Eventually, Jordan allowed herself to be escorted, zombie-like, to another room, where she met the nurse who would conduct her exam. The stark, fluorescent-lit room had an air of quiet calm that did nothing to dispel her gloom. She continued to sit speechlessly, with the exception of answering the questions directed at her.

When the nurse began the vaginal exam, Jordan couldn't help but grimace at the light touches that ghosted over the raw, tender tissue there. When she was told that there were several abrasions, she was thrust into a still deeper shock, but aside from the injection she was given to prevent infection, she remained in a detached stupor.

Finally the exam was over, and Jordan was led to a small room, after being told that a police officer was there to speak with her. She closed her eyes in an effort to drown out the events of the last several hours and eventually dozed off, only to be awakened by the same officer she had briefly observed at her apartment earlier.

He asked her several questions that she dispassionately answered. He seemed to grow increasingly frustrated with her when she couldn't keep her eyes from closing. "Miss Smithson!" he snapped. "How the hell am I supposed to investigate a so-called 'rape' when you can't even see fit to keep your eyes open long enough to talk to me?"

The officer's raised voice caused Jordan's head to jolt upward just in time to see the back of him as he steamrolled from her room. However, before the door had completely closed, Sam angrily stomped in. Jordan was astounded when she furiously exclaimed, "That goddamn bastard! He would have a hard time staying awake too if he took Phenergan. What an asshole!"

Sam bent down to help Jordan to her feet. "Come on. I'll take you home." Jordan could hear her mumbling under her breath. "Fucking small town cops. What a prick!"

By the time they reached Sam's car, Jordan was fighting the pull on her eyelids. After settling into the passenger seat, she laid her head on the door and fell asleep.

Chapter Eight

On Wednesday, the city gradually began to thaw as a warm front moved in around noon. Though schools were still closed for the day, many commuters were out and about, running errands, or heading to jobs that had been neglected for several days. Morgan was one of the latter, and although she had greatly enjoyed the time she'd spent with John, she was ready to return to some semblance of normalcy. After checking with John and assuring that Lucia felt comfortable with the arrangement, she left her child there with plans to return that evening.

Morgan was working at her desk when an email from the title company popped up with a meeting time for Patrick to close on the house across from John's. Excitedly, she phoned Jasmine to share the good news. Looking at her watch, she realized that the appointment was only a few hours away.

As luck would have it, the winter storm had left Morgan's schedule open for the day. Considering that Mag's mom's funeral was the following day, she was thankful, as she planned to take that day off. When she finished relaying the details of the appointment to Patrick, she hung up and went in search of her boss.

"I hear you did it again, champ!" he congratulated, referring to her closing of the million dollar house. "And at list price, too… this guy have a hard-on for you, girlie?" he chided.

Morgan felt herself blushing as she remembered her first encounter with Patrick. She shut down that line of thinking quickly, however, as she contemplated all of the relationships of the involved parties.

In an attempt to head off further comments of that nature, Morgan cleared her throat and said, somewhat crossly, "Well, I *am* a professional, Mack. Give me some credit." She had meant to be stern, but her comment came across harsher than intended, so she quickly added, "I think he was just really interested in it. His brother lives across the street."

Unphased by her rudeness, Mack raised his coffee cup to her in appreciation. "I've got to hand it to you, lady! Even in the midst of a blizzard, you're still making record sales!" She smiled in response to the compliment and answered casually, "That's just how I roll, Mack." The two then enjoyed a celebratory toast from the bottle of Dom Perignon that he kept in his mini-fridge for such occasions.

As they sat in companionable silence, she thought of the upcoming funeral. She then informed Mack that her kids would be returning soon.

He chuckled, "Wait, let me guess: you think I should give you the rest of the week off?" Morgan knew he was teasing her, as her job didn't truly require her to be present in the office. Playing along, she feigned a desperate plea. "Oh, pretty please, boss...I'll love you forever if you do."

He grunted, letting out a small chuckle. "If I did that, then what am I supposed to do all alone in the office for the next couple of days?"

Morgan cocked her eyebrow in response and stared at him. "Well, you *could* sale a house for once, instead of leaving all of the grunt work to your slaves," she grinned playfully.

"Touché, champ!" he enthusiastically replied, raising his glass and lightly clinking it against hers. They talked briefly about Morgan's recent successes, as well as her close calls, until Mack's wife called.

He answered the phone sweetly. "Hello, my beautiful Amber! I couldn't wait to talk to you either!" Morgan was slightly shocked at the sappy tone he used, and continued to gawk at him as he talked. Finally, he told Amber, "My dear, give me a just moment. I have an important client that I need to send away." With that, he put the phone on hold and turned to Morgan. "I'm not a dick *all* the time," he pointed out, defending himself in response to her confused expression.

Hurrying to drink the last of her champagne, Morgan stood in preparation to leave and turned toward the door of his office. "Okay, I'll see you next week, bossman." He nodded in agreement, and she gathered her things before leaving for the appointment with Patrick at the title company.

****

Awakening in the sprawling bed that she had occupied for the last several days, Maggie felt a glowing warmth that permeated her from the marrow of her bones to the silky ends of her crimson curls. Sensing her surroundings, she could feel Shannon stretched out behind her, enveloping her with his arms and legs entwined around hers, holding them securely together.

When she moved, Shannon stirred, pulling her impossibly closer. Simultaneously, he gently rasped his five o'clock shadow against her neck, while twirling a massage over one of her nipples that was within easy access. When Maggie's breath hissed audibly, his grip tightened, and in one smooth motion, he rolled her over him, and then settled himself on top of her, leaving them both breathless.

His lips descended onto hers, and their tongues danced an intimate tango, each dipping in and around in exploration of the other, while their hands roamed. In no time, they were both incredibly aroused, involuntarily thrusting their hips into each other, until his hand found her wrists and pulled them over her head.

She looked up at him, taken aback at the sudden maneuver. "I wanna dominate ye now, Maggie. Will ye let me do that to ya?"

Her cheeks reddened from his question, as much as from his rapid shifting of their bodies that brought them to their current position. As Shannon awaited her response, he twisted one of her nipples between his fingers with his free hand, causing her to arch upward into him. Maggie nodded. He smiled slightly mischievously, enjoying the feel of Maggie's light thrusts, which rubbed him in just the right spot, causing his erection to lengthen and stiffen.

What happened next caught Maggie off-guard, as she had always believed she possessed a better-than-average awareness of her surroundings. Reaching across the bed, Shannon took two small silk cords from under the pillow he had lain his head on. Retaining one of her wrists, he deftly slipped the cord over the other and tied her to the bed post. He then repeated this with her other wrist, leaving her arms spread, immobile yet comfortable, above her head.

Once he had her secure, Shannon settled his weight onto his knees, straddling her legs. "There," he said with satisfaction. "That's much better." He nodded and smiled as he looked her over, as if admiring his handiwork.

Maggie's curiosity was piqued, as was her excitement, and she couldn't wait to see what Shannon intended to do to her.

Watching him study her so intently caused her to again become flushed, and she wriggled futilely in response.

Noting her struggle, Shannon's grin broadened, and he captured her gaze with his before revealing his objective. "I'll not let ye go 'til I've had me pleasure from ye, lil' lass." With this promise, he leaned forward and rubbed his shaft between her legs, causing her to gyrate wildly, desperately wanting to feel him inside of her. "Not yet," he told her, as he pulled back.

"What are you going to do to me?" Maggie's question came out in a hoarse whisper

"Ye'll have ter wait ye're turn to see, *mo ghra*," Shannon winked. With this said, his mouth descended to her core, and he lapped up her sweet juices; slowly at first, heightening the intense throbbing that pulsed between her legs.

Maggie couldn't keep from bucking her hips in response to the pleasure he was creating. However, her movements caused the friction to increase to a blazing crescendo that had her dizzy and panting.

Shannon studied Maggie's face as her head whipped from side to side in ecstasy. When she was on the verge of exploding in his mouth, he suddenly halted his rhythmic oral massage, sitting up to observe the flushed thrall he had created.

Her hips swiveled and lifted wildly off of the mattress, in an effort to get what she wanted from him. "Why did you stop?" she demanded breathlessly.

Shannon smiled knowingly. "Because I needed te see this look on ye're face o' ye wantin' me so badly, cara." Sliding through her silken folds, he entered her with his fingers, reveling in her wet-hot slipperiness. Soon, his strokes became faster and firmer, and she moaned in time with his thrusts.

"That's right love; let go. I want ter see ye're face when ye squirt ye're delicious juices all over me fingers and bathe them in ye're slick heat." His demand was all it took to pull the orgasm from her, and the hot jets of her release spewed out. She settled back onto the pillow in satisfied exhaustion. Shannon traced his fingers to her inner thighs, collecting the cream she had emitted there, and brought it to his mouth, suckling her essence from his fingertips.

As Maggie sighed contentedly, Shannon pondered what to do with her next. When she began to stir, he again reached under the pillow from where he had retrieved the cords. When he lifted it, she saw a cache of unfamiliar items.

"What's all this?" she asked, still breathless.

Smiling in anticipation of using the items on her, Shannon informed her, "Ye'll see. Donut worry, lass, ye'll see right good and love it by the time I'm through with ye." She tingled with excitement, thoroughly titillated by the array of items displayed. His hand hovered above them, as if by close proximity he would choose the favored toy.

Finally, his hand stilled over a pair of some type of metal clamps that had speckled feathers at one end. "Mph!" He made a sound in the back of his throat as he picked them up. Captivated, she watched him, the suspense adding to her excitement.

He held them in his closed hand as he settled over her, straddling her hips. Staring down at her, his mouth curled up at the corner. She realized that he knew exactly what he was doing to her as her eyes widened and her breath quickened, Shannon taking great delight in the mounting pleasure he was creating.

Slowly, he reached down with one of the clamps and gently placed it on her nipple. The sensation was slightly painful at first, but then changed to a heated stirring sensation that radiated deeply, where his fingers had just been. He paused briefly to gauge her reaction. Satisfied, he placed the second clamp on her other nipple, causing her hips to lift slightly, until they met with the resistance of his body weight.

Shannon's grin widened so that he resembled the Cheshire cat, and he bent over her to whisper in her ear. "That's right, *mo shearc*, feel the pleasure I make for ye." He followed his statement with a nip of her ear, and then twirled his tongue around it, causing a tingle of pleasure to shoot through her.

When her hips jerked off of the bed that time, they went higher as he had lifted himself up slightly to whisper in her ear. Maggie's movement caused her to grind against his swollen, throbbing shaft. Maggie was so frenzied. He had to enter her. *Now.*

Parting her thighs with his body, he settled close to her and then with a swiftness that attested to the ferocity of his intensifying desire, he pounded into her. As he thrust to meet her, she thrust her hips to accept him. The movement caused the nipple clamps to shift, resulting in an orgasm that ripped through her, exploding with a force that had her seeing stars and moaning loudly.

Her response, as well as the hot cream that pooled around Shannon's engorged organ where it entered her, had his climax spewing from his loins with an expulsive dynamism that filled her. He then collapsed on top of her. The clamps dug into the flesh of Maggie's breasts, but she was so caught up that she didn't notice, or care, for the time.

When the post-coital bliss had worn off, she moved, causing the tissue under the clamps to sting. Shannon had to feel them and hear her groan. He shifted his position so that he was lying beside her. Reaching over, he unclamped her nipples one at a time, released her from her silken tethers, and pulled her close.

After cuddling together for some time, Maggie moved so that she could see him more fully. The lovers gazed into each other's eyes. Their eye contact was interrupted by Shannon leaning in and kissing her on the mouth; slowly at first, but then it deepened so that they were all but devouring each other.

They were becoming increasingly turned on, and Maggie thought for sure that they were heading in the direction of making love again. Instead, they were interrupted by the bedroom door suddenly swinging open, so hard that it crashed into the wall behind it. Maggie sat up with a start, watching as an infuriated blonde-haired woman stalked angrily toward the bed.

Shannon jumped from Maggie's side and quickly moved to intercept the hysterical woman, who was clearly hell-bent on physically assaulting Maggie. Like the proverbial deer in headlights, Maggie could think to do nothing other than stare in shock at the scene that played out in front of her, struggling to process what she was seeing.

Vaguely, she could hear Shannon yelling, "Siobhan, what in bloody hell are ye doin' here?" before she heard skin slapping skin. Looking at the struggling couple, Maggie saw that the intruder was slapping Shannon hard, and repeatedly, anywhere on his unclothed body that she was able to reach while avoiding his effort to stop her.

Remembering the physical violence she had suffered at the hands of her grandmother, Maggie reacted instinctively, moving as if by an unseen force to the debacle. Reaching up, she snagged a generous handful of the woman's blonde hair. After finally dragging the woman off of her looming, red-headed lover, Maggie pulled her to the floor where she pummeled her several times with her fists.

As the melee continued, Shannon stood as if numb and too stunned to move. In the confines of the room, the scene was chaotic. Siobhan appeared helpless under Maggie's relentless onslaught, merely lying on the floor, being straddled and beaten. Maggie was saying incomprehensible things that came out as little more than a string of slurred words, clumps of hair on the floor close to Siobhan's ear; locks that must have settled there when she was originally dragged down.

Taking it all in, Shannon appeared to just avoid laughing as he watched his naked lover assaulting his wife. Maggie seemed a fantasy; ethereal, appearing a wild goddess defending her god.

The words that finally spurned him to action came from Siobhan's mouth: "…hurting the babby." If Maggie hadn't already been backing away from her, those words would have been extremely obscene in the quiet of the room. As it was, Shannon leaned down to assist his distraught wife to a standing position. Siobhan seized the opportunity to latch onto him, hoisting herself into his arms.

"She was tryin' ter kill yer wee babby, Shannon!" the woman shrieked frantically, glaring down at Maggie. She then began sobbing uncontrollably into his shoulder. Shannon looked helplessly at Maggie where she was sitting on the floor, leaning against the wall.

Drained from the emotional and physical burden, coupled with the depletion of the adrenaline stores she had just exhausted, Maggie rested her head on her knees, wrapping her arms around them. As Shannon silently helped his frenzied wife out of the room, Maggie watched from her peripheral vision until the door closed softly behind them.

Without warning, Maggie's body began trembling violently. After picking herself up off the floor, she slowly moved around the room in an effort to dress herself. Once she managed to find acceptable clothing, she stepped tentatively into the hall. To her dismay, she could still hear wailing that seemed to come from somewhere downstairs. Not one to shirk her responsibilities, she walked in the direction of the weeping with a sigh.

At the head of the stairs, she looked down and was able to see the commotion taking place below. The blonde woman, whom Maggie was certain was Shannon's wife, was sitting in the chair that occupied the entryway, still sobbing, and looking quite forlorn. Maggie was having a difficult time understanding her speech, but she could see that Shannon was not; neither was John, who had apparently also been pulled into the turmoil.

Maggie had been observing the three for a few moments before it hit her: they weren't speaking English. Though she couldn't understand the words, the body language between the two men suggested sympathy for the distressed, tearful woman in the chair. When Siobhan eventually looked up and noticed Maggie standing at the top of the stairs, she dissolved into another torrent of sobs and moans. These were accentuated by the apprehensive expressions on the faces of Shannon and John, when they also looked up.

With that, Maggie turned abruptly and returned to the guest room, slamming the door behind her. Secluded in her room, she angrily began flinging her belongings into her bag. When she was nearly packed, the door flew open and Shannon stood in the doorway. She stopped briefly, looking at him with a combination of fear, sadness, and anger.

Shannon's face was expressionless, and Maggie couldn't decide what, if anything, he planned to say or do. Eventually, he entered the room, closing the door behind him and, with an exasperated sigh, sat down heavily on the bed. His shoulders were slumped, and he looked defeated. Despite everything that had just transpired, Maggie desperately wanted to comfort him but didn't; unsure of how he would respond.

Instead, she walked over to the bed and stood in front of him; close enough that he knew she was there, yet just out of reach in case he had physical violence in mind, perhaps retribution for her assault of his apparently-pregnant wife. Finally he moved, slowly at first, and Maggie felt her heart jump into her throat. When he raised his arms to wrap them around her waist, pulling her close and resting his head against her belly, she let out a long breath and relaxed.

Her hands moved to the top of his head, caressing him and holding him to her. She began to feel wetness on her abdomen, and realized that he was crying. The lump that developed in her throat nearly choked her. Maggie became aware of the subtle movements of his shoulders as he cried into her. She alternated between rubbing his back and running her fingers through his thick hair in an attempt to soothe him.

Finally, he released his hold on her waist and looked up at her. Maggie noticed that the tears that shimmered in his brown eyes highlighted their beautiful color. Her heart ached for him.

When he spoke, his voice sounded more like a croak, and the words he said were the last thing she ever thought she would hear. "I must return home, me love." She stared down at him in shock, a sinking feeling in the pit of her stomach.

The grief Shannon felt was reflected in Maggie's eyes. Needing to feel her closer, he pulled her onto his lap so that she was straddling him. Shannon kissed Maggie passionately, pouring into it every bit of his heart and soul in an attempt to convey his feelings. As he reflected, he thought, *nay*! He didna want her to feel the heartache he felt, which was as though his chest was being ripped open and his heart viciously cut out.

"I want ye so much, me love. These last days ha' been heaven…for it to end li' this, 'tis…unthinkable." She stopped his words with a kiss of her own, pushing him onto the bed. Her lusty passion was felt from the intimate caresses on his chin and shoulders, as well as the soft swipes of her tongue between his lips, and then down his chest.

When he felt Maggie's tantalizing tongue moving toward his groin, he objected. "Nay, ye canna do that, cara. I need ter taste ye meself just now so tha' I willna forget the flavor of ye when ye have gone."

Maggie halted her downward path, thoughtful for a moment. Finally, she came up with a compromise. Without saying a word, she turned to lie on her side, pulling him so that they each had oral access to the other's nether regions. Shannon devoured her like a starving animal, rubbing his chin on her so that his entire face beneath his nose was covered in Maggie's luscious juices.

No sooner did they suckle each other vigorously several times than they each climaxed explosively into the other's eagerly awaiting mouth. Shannon had to catch his breath for a moment as he rested his head on her thigh. He then exclaimed through gritted teeth, "Mmmph! Maggie, 'tis nay enough. I must have ye again! Maggie, can I have ye now?"

In silent response, she moved so that she was lying next to him and once in place, pulled him on top of her. He was already aroused, and his pulsating shaft entered her with such a force that it had them both moving up the bed, creating slapping sounds with each thrust. These were intermingled with moans and grunts of desire. Finally, he spent himself into her, and they both lay still, exhausted, taking in each other's scent.

Eventually, Shannon stood up and dressed. After standing over her and studying her wistfully, he leaned over Maggie, kissing her lips and explaining, "Tis me wife, lass. She ha' come to bring me back." Maggie stared at him, trying to absorb the situation which, evidently, suddenly required his return.

As if reading her mind, he continued. "She is wi' child, love, and a right dangerous pregnancy 'tis for her. If she loses the wee one this early, I mus' be there. 'Tis bad luck otherwise, and if I donut have nay to do wi' it, when I could ha', 'tis even worse so."

She mulled over this information, as confused expressions chased across her face. He sensed this and elaborated. "Ye see, we Irish, we're a right superstitious lot, but ye ha' to be understandin', dem auld tales ha' been proved time an' again. 'Tis madness to no listen to 'em."

Maggie was intrigued by his talk of old beliefs and superstitions, but it was overshadowed by the excruciating grief she felt at losing him. She actually felt that his absence would be far more painful than that of her mother. Not that her attachment to him in any way compared to the attachment she had for her mother. It didn't. But by the end, her mom had become so demented that there had been little interaction aside from the medical care Maggie provided. She had often wondered if it would have been more merciful if her mother had passed much sooner.

Shannon's grunt brought Maggie back to the present moment, and she shot up, embracing him and pulling him in for a last kiss. His words, although spoken with an almost fanatical excitement, held a note of finality, and she knew that it was the last she would see of him.

When she went to release Shannon, he wouldn't let go, and instead increased his grip on her. His breath in her hair became more erratic and as he held her tighter, she wondered if he would ever let her go.

Finally he did, but only to scoop her up and carry her back to the bed. He set her down so that she was bent over, facing away from him. She expected him to enter her at any moment with a breathtaking force. Instead, she felt his hands on either side of her hips. She closed her eyes to fully experience the sensations as his hands moved softly up and down her back, causing her to shiver and moan with pleasure.

Suddenly, his hands stopped their ceaseless roaming, and she thought that he was withdrawing from her. A profound sadness swept over her when she realized that she would never again feel him touching her or making love to her. Furthermore, she was certain that it would never be as good with another person as long as she lived.

Maggie's thoughts were abruptly interrupted when she felt a sharp sting on her buttock. She realized with a loud cry that Shannon had bitten her there. She tried desperately to escape but he held on, clamping a death grip onto her gluteal muscle with his teeth. When yelping and wiggling proved ineffective against his vice-like hold, she resigned herself to the fact that she was stuck in her predicament. However, she slowly realized that the sensation, although painful, was not necessarily upleasant. Soon, she noticed that where she had before felt pain, she now felt his tongue swirling over the tender skin, inducing a tingling sensation and the notion of being branded. The idea turned her on immensely.

Finally, she felt Shannon move and after he shifted, his body blanketed hers so that they were spooning, prone. He again caressed her with his hands, so gently that she wondered at times if she had imagined what had just happened. Eventually, he repositioned himself so that he was still lying on top of her but had himself lifted up, hovering over her so that she could barely feel his body, other than his weight on the mattress on either side of her. She thought that surely he meant to go, and silently prepared herself for the grief that she knew would soon follow.

Maggie was completely unprepared for what he did next. With a suddenness that left her little time to ready herself, Shannon devoured the skin on her shoulder, causing her to cry out in pain. She held perfectly still, somehow aware that the slightest movement on her part would do more harm than good, and allowed him free reign in how he chose to handle her body.

After several seconds of intense pressure, his hold gradually lessened, and he lapped at her with his tongue, leaving her with a feeling of warmth and a longing for what he would give her. His touches gradually became lighter, until she again could no longer feel his presence, other than his ever-present weight on the mattress.

She tried to guess the next place he would touch her and to her surprise, found that she was quite excited to be bitten by him again. Her prediction proved to be wrong again, however, when she felt him grip her hips and then enter her, leaving her immediately moaning and breathless.

As the beginning thrusts took place, she thought that surely he would take her quickly and furiously-as his passion seemed to goad him into doing-so that he built the pressure to an overwhelming wave of pleasure, leaving them both disintegrating and panting.

Very quickly, however, she realized that this time was different. He was taking his time with her, drawing it out. As soon as one of them began moaning loudly or breathing heavily, he slowed his thrusts, almost teasingly.

At one point, he stopped altogether, pulling her to sit on his lap, although he remained inside of her while he did this. She didn't know why he positioned them in such an awkward way, but when he stroked small circular caresses over her nipples and whispered loving sentiments in her ear, she knew he was wanting to savor their connection for as long as possible. In fact, he said to her during this, "I want to remember ye just like this for always, *mo graw*, and I'ma sure I couldna get enough of ye ever, even if I tried." Maggie closed her eyes to the emotions that threatened to overwhelm her and decided that, at least for now, she would live fully in the moment, enjoying every touch, and regret the loss later.

After he made his declaration, she turned her face to his and took his mouth in hers. Their tongues dipped and twirled, until they both inevitably became turned on once more. Eventually, he lifted her, replacing her in front of him on her hands and knees.

Initially after the heated kiss, he had driven into her repeatedly, faster and harder, but as their pleasure escalated, he slowed the pace to a more leisurely one, again drawing out their ecstasy. He rocked in and out of her for a while, until even the slow strokes had him moaning as he watched himself enter her. He leaned down and kissed her lips, biting the lower one, and then picked up the pace. Their combined moaning echoed throughout the room like a symphony of carnal joy. It crested into one final loud, heartfelt moan. Maggie wasn't sure if it came from Shannon or herself, but knew that she had to lay still holding him inside, fearing the inevitably looming loss.

****

Jordan awakened to the relentless buzzing of her alarm, peeking through her eyelid just enough to see that it was two in the afternoon. Remembering the previous day's ordeal, she groaned and quickly swallowed to keep the tears at bay. She turned her head in an attempt to locate her phone, causing the ache in her head to increase from a dull buzz to a deafening roar.

After swallowing several more times, she felt for her phone, squinted as she dialed her work and, eyes closed, brought the phone to her ear.

"Five west, this is Ashley, how can I direct your call?" The overly-cheerful unit coordinator made her head hurt even more, and she could feel the bile begin to rise. "Can I help you? Hello?" the voice asked.

Finally, she managed to get her voice to function. "It's Jordan. Can I speak with the charge?" Her voice was hoarse and sounded foreign to her own ears. After a brief pause, the voice responded, "One moment; I'll transfer you."

After three rings, Jordan heard the voice of the person she least wanted to talk to. "If you're calling in, think again, Smithson," Mary, the charge nurse, threatened. Jordan had to swallow before she could respond, but was finally able to form a few words. "Can't work today...sick," Jordan said weakly into the phone.

Jordan was aware of an exaggerated, impatient sigh into the phone, and Mary warned, "You know you're on thin ice already, Smithson. I'll put you down, even though I shouldn't. The *policy*," she snarled, accentuating each syllable, "is that you give at least two hours' notice when you call in." Jordan thought the nasty woman might have said more, but closed her phone before she could hear any of it.

Struggling, she reached for the prescription bottle on the nightstand next to her bed. When she finally managed to get it open, she poured several pills onto the mattress next to her. After a few tries, she scooped some up and dropped them into her mouth. Thankful that the hospital had given her a prescription for Valium, she swallowed and managed to gulp enough water so that they stayed put.

Numbly, she assumed that she had ingested maybe three or four Valium and closed her eyes, hoping that the sweet oblivion of sleep would overtake her before she puked again. Fifteen minutes later, her wish was granted.

Chapter Nine

Hours later, Maggie and Shannon awakened, in an intimate skin-to-skin embrace, to the feel of Morgan shaking them. "Maggie, I didn't see you at dinner and I was worried," she told her friend. Maggie smelled alcohol on her breath and at second glance, it was obvious that she was excited about something.

As if reading her mind, which wasn't too far-fetched considering how close they were, Morgan blurted out the good news. "Patrick closed on his house today!"

Maggie lifted her head slightly, nodding in understanding, but then replaced it on Shannon's shoulder when she felt him pulling her closer to him with an unintelligible mumble. His subconscious possession of her brought a smile to Maggie's face. She was briefly lost in the bliss of the moment until she remembered Morgan was standing there. "What time is it?" she yawned.

"Seven-thirty." Before she even had a chance to ask about Shannon's wife, Morgan answered her question. "Oh by the way, John sent cray-cray to a hotel for the night after he promised her that Shannon would be there by eleven tomorrow morning to accompany her to the airport."

Roused by the mention of his name, Shannon tightened his hold on Maggie, peeking out over her nest of curly locks to confirm what he had heard. "Eh? Me wife is gone fer the night, ye say?"

Morgan seemed startled by his responsiveness; after all, he had seemed nearly unconscious mere seconds earlier. Recovering gracefully, she told him, "Right. She's staying over at the Hilton. John and Patrick finally calmed her down and Jasmine convinced her to take a sedative. Then, when they reassured her that you would meet her in the morning, she agreed to let John put her up in a room for the night."

Maggie tried to see Shannon's face in an attempt to read his expression, but he held her too closely and she was unable to change position. It seemed to Maggie that his grip on her strengthened when his wife was the topic of conversation, but she ultimately dismissed it as being her imagination.

"Hmph," he grumbled. "Tha' sounds jus' like 'er. Give'r a royal dwellin' an' she'll be a'stayin' any place ye put 'er. The more ye be doin' wi' the fru-fru, the more she do be a'sniffin' fer ya." His cynicism was unmistakable, as was the feel of his hand clutched between Maggie's legs, and she thought that it seemed almost like a defensive gesture.

In light of Shannon's demeanor, as well as the intimate position in which her best friend was entangled, Morgan cleared her throat and turned to leave, but not before announcing, "Anyway, I just came up here to let you guys know that we're downstairs celebrating Patrick's house, and we'd love to have y'all join us!"

Morgan was almost to the door when Patrick responded. "We'll be down in a bit, lass. For now, I need to enjoy me lover." His voice trailed off with his face nuzzled in Maggie's neck and his hand burrowed between her thighs.

As soon as the door closed behind Morgan, Shannon gently turned Maggie's face toward his and brought his lips to hers, making love to her mouth with his tongue while his hands eagerly explored her body. He seemed pleased that she was so receptive to his touch as he stroked her nipples. He kissed her and lightly circled the stiffening pink buds with his fingertips, as her hips arched upward into him and she cried out.

"Mmm, Maggie, I love that ye're so responsive to me, lass," he whispered as he began kissing his way down her body, beginning at the hollow of her collar bone and descending to her hip, exploring with his mouth. He smiled up at her before swiftly parting her thighs and burying his face below the red curly hairs nestled there.

Maggie's hands made their way of their own volition to tangle in his hair as she anchored herself to his mouth so that she could ride the waves of pleasure at a pace suited to her longings. He allowed this for a bit, but then began to devour her. He clamped his mouth onto her as his forearm came to rest across her hips to hold her still. When she realized his intent, Maggie couldn't take it anymore.

"Please!" she begged, as he tasted her essence and penetrated her with his tongue. The pleasure was so intense that it was almost painful, and she continued to plead with him. "Please, Shannon, it's too much. I can't take it!" He smiled, obviously enjoying seeing the erotic torture he was inflicting upon her. Finally, he released the hold he had with his mouth to study her. His halted progress allowed her to relax enough so that her fists released the sheets, and her head ceased whipping side to side on the pillow.

At long last, Shannon slowly entered her. She responded by meeting his thrusts with her hips and wrapping her legs around his waist to pull him deeper inside of her.

As he thrust into her, she watched him through the slits in her barely-open eyes. She noticed every detail of the beauty and grace of his movements and burnt his image into her memory for all time. He was watching her as well; perhaps for the same reason, but also to assess her response to him, as he seemed to be so receptive to it.

When an involuntary moan escaped her throat and she lifted herself up to meet him, he sensed that it was time and let himself go. Spending himself into her, he surged forward as she clawed his arms in the fervor of her thrall. With an exhausted sigh, she settled back, pulling him to rest on top of her.

They knew their time together was limited. It seemed that Shannon didn't want to waste a single moment as he caressed her cheek and then kissed her. Maggie returned his affection, knowing that it was possible they would end up in the throes of passion again. However, the kiss they shared became tender and intimate in a different way.

He finished with his lips softly pressed against hers and his hands gently cradling her head. Withdrawing from her mouth, he rubbed his head against her chest, holding her to him as if attempting to ensure he would always remember the scent and feel of her. If his wife had anything to do with it, Maggie knew that this visit to the States would be his last; if his actions were any indicator, he clearly wanted to bask in its sanctuary for as long as possible.

Their short-lived union was coming to an end. Maggie wanted to convey to Shannon that she accepted him and that she supported him in his plight. She enjoyed his presence and held him to her, caressing his back and hair, as her face turned to the top of his head and she breathed in his scent. Owing to the fact that her time with him was quickly running out, and once he departed it would be the last she would ever see of him, she was determined to make the most of every minute.

After holding each other close for a long while, the two gradually began to stir in unison, moving slowly to dress for the festivities taking place downstairs. They stole shy glances at each other occasionally, which led to coy smiles and soft giggles.

Once they were dressed, they walked toward the door together arm in arm, sauntered down the hallway, and made their way down the stairs. Loud voices echoed throughout the house, and there were shouts intermingled with raucous laughter.

When they emerged in the kitchen, they discovered that the atmosphere was quite festive, indeed. There were shot glasses lined up on the edge of the island, and it appeared as though several rounds of shots had already been consumed, as a cache of half-empty liquor bottles adorned the kitchen countertop behind the partygoers.

To Maggie's surprise, the old woman was there as well, and she appeared much livelier than when Mag had first seen her. At the present moment, she was waddling around the kitchen, flapping her arms as if they were wings, and making a high-pitched squawking sound. Maggie realized, with no small amount of amusement, that she was doing an imitation of a duck.

"The love birds finally join us!" Patrick said in response to seeing the two enter.

"Hmph!" Shannon grunted at the comment, wrapping his arm around Maggie's waist, and ushering her into the kitchen. "A game o' Cock's Walk, is it, then?" Shannon proposed, taking in Brunne's activities along with the half-empty liquor bottles.

"Yeah, mate. You in?" affirmed Patrick. Shannon took the challenge, inviting Maggie to join them. "Jus' sit back an' watch, me love," he told her as he stepped up to the kitchen island.

Maggie's fondness of being in the thick of things was nothing compared to her curiosity of seeing the group in action, and she eagerly seated herself on the counter in an effort to take in as much of it as she could.

Eventually, Brunne stopped and then stood abruptly, grasping the countertop for support when she began to sway.

"What's next, Ma?" John asked, and everyone looked to her expectantly. She let out a loud and deep belch, announcing, "Scotch; we do scotch next. Is good fer da heart, no?"

"Scotch it tis, and the next loser is the cock." John turned to Maggie. "Will you be judge, my dear? Some people…" he chided, elbowing his brother roughly in the ribs, "…like to cheat."

Maggie agreed and settled against the cupboard, ready to watch the action. Patrick retrieved a shot glass from behind him while Jasmine doled out the scotch, leaving each glass two-thirds full. Morgan set one in front of each person surrounding the kitchen's center island, and the room grew quiet.

Finally, Brunne made her quacking sound three times, and each person drank, in an effort to avoid being last. The men were first to finish, and slammed their glasses down in unison. Brunne was next, and Maggie figured she probably had plenty of practice drinking shots. As the two younger women competitively sipped the amber liquid, Maggie could see that it was a losing battle for her best friend, as she started sputtering after each swallow.

Her hunch was confirmed when Morgan choked, regurgitating the contents onto the countertop and back into the glass. As John pounded her on the back to induce oxygen flow, Jasmine finished hers, making Morgan the loser. When she finally caught her breath, she looked up at John and smiled sheepishly, and the two began giggling intimately.

After a few moments when Maggie could see that her friend was preparing herself, Morgan nodded her head, as if to herself, and then lifted herself onto the center island. The group watched in fascination as she tucked her hands into her armpits and flapped her arms. She then extended her head as far as her neck would allow, and began to crow quite convincingly. She jumped down onto the floor and began "pecking" John's shoulder, while continuing to cluck at him.

Maggie thought surely he would become annoyed with her, but instead he whipped around quickly so that his lips caught hers during one of her downward pecking swipes, and he picked her up, placing her back on the top of the island, so that she was level with his mouth. Suddenly, the entire group burst into applause, and though their kiss lingered a few moments longer, they finally broke off, smiling, and looking slightly embarrassed.

"Great game ye played, e'rybody!" concluded Patrick, before turning to intimately kiss Jasmine on the mouth.

By this time, Brunne was all but swaying, and with another hearty belch announced, "Is time I made it to me bed, ye wee scoundrels." As she was leaving, she passed by Shannon and paused for a moment. Suddenly, she leaned into him and placed a heavy, passionate kiss on his lips. He appeared shocked. So shocked, in fact, that he stood frozen as she embraced him. The others watched in stunned silence as well. Finally, she released him, and with a satisfied, "Hmph!" she sighed, "I been wantin' ter do that fer a long while, lad!" Then, apropos of nothing, she shuffled through the door that led to the study, retiring to her quarters for the evening.

Shannon stood as tensely as a statue, eyes wide, staring into space, trying to process what had just happened. For several minutes, the atmosphere was one of hushed awe, but the tension was broken when Shannon remarked, "Weel, I didna expect tha' to happen," with an embarrassed chuckle.

His words mobilized everyone, including Shannon himself, who wrapped his arms around Maggie and buried his face in her neck. She wasn't sure if it was for reassurance, or to conceal the awkwardness he felt. When she saw in her peripheral vision that the tips of his ears were a bright crimson, she decided it was probably the latter.

Patrick gathered Jasmine into his arms and whispered in her ear, "I think it's time we made our way home too, love. I've been dyin' ter spend the first night in our new home wit' ye." She kissed him zealously on the mouth in response.

When she finally broke away from him, she looked to John and asked, "Do you mind keeping the girls over here tonight?"

Morgan's arms were around John's neck and his back was to her. Maggie noticed that John had seemed to tense up at the question, and it appeared as though Morgan held him firmly to her. *Probably to keep him from overreacting to his wife's question,* Maggie guessed, as she recalled how John had recently snapped at his wife in the very same room in which they stood. Before he could answer, Morgan volunteered, "We'd be more than happy to keep the girls. You two go on and enjoy your first night in the new house."

Maggie couldn't help but notice John's hands pinching Morgan's bottom in response to her offer. She was unsure whether Jasmine had noticed the interplay, but decided that it didn't matter, when Jasmine smiled brightly at Morgan's hospitality, hugging her tightly and kissing her lips. "Thank you so much, Morgan...and John." She muttered his name, and quickly gave him an awkward hug.

Before John could respond, Jasmine and Patrick walked out of the kitchen, arm in arm, kissing intermittently, appearing to be in their own little world. Maggie noticed Morgan watching them with a thoughtful smile as they left. She thought back to the conversation Morgan had confided she'd had with John when he had decided to peaceably step aside in order to permit his wife to be with his brother. She knew Morgan had had her doubts, but seeing the two together clearly seemed to instill in her a sense of peace, and surely it had quelled her insecurities about their current situation which allowed Morgan to be with Jasmine's husband.

"Eh?" John repeated, prompting Morgan to focus on him.

Her self-conscious smile communicated what everyone was likely thinking- that her dulled wit was probably from the alcohol. As if to clear her head, she shook it, asking, "I'm sorry, what?"

He smiled at her in his way, while tucking loose strands of hair behind her ears, repeating his question. "What time is your friend's wake tomorrow?"

His question was sobering, and she responded, "Oh, I'd almost forgotten about that. It's at…" She seemed to labor at grasping the query, but Maggie piped up. "One. It's at one o'clock."

After he kissed Morgan lovingly on the mouth, John looked her in the eye. "I wanted to go with you, if that's okay, love." He kissed her once more before rephrasing, "Is it okay if I go with you?"

Morgan was dumbfounded. Maggie knew she was taken aback by his request, and that she probably loved the idea of him being there with her and supporting her. After returning his kiss, Morgan answered him. "Oh my gosh. I would *love* that. Maggie? That okay with you?" She asked this without turning to look at her friend; instead, maintaining her gaze into John's eyes. She appeared so lost in him that she was surprised when her friend sincerely replied, "Of course. I'm so glad you'll have him there with you, Morgan." Most of what Maggie said seemed lost on Morgan, as mesmerized by John as she was.

Maggie watched the two lovers embrace with a bone-deep longing that revealed just how lonely she had become. She began to ponder the affair she had been recently enjoying with her own lover, and the cliché "better to have loved and lost than never to have loved at all" came to mind. The time she had spent with Shannon made her feel deeply loved, and she doubted she would ever regret it. With a detached numbness, she resigned herself to the fact that she was okay with losing him. She knew, while watching her best friend lost in her lover, that although she might face a solitary future, she was grateful for the touch she had so thoroughly relished, and knew that she would cherish its memory always. The warmth she gleaned from these memories were already giving her assurance that she would never feel alone again.

When she turned away from Morgan and John, her eyes automatically found Shannon's, and she could see her own emotions mirrored in his eyes. Their gaze locked until he came closer, holding her in a tight embrace. It was so tight, in fact, that Maggie had difficulty breathing, but then decided it didn't matter because she was holding her breath anyway.

She was carried away in the moment, with Shannon's body smothering her, until she felt Morgan's soft lips on her forehead. "We're going up to bed, Mag. Get some rest and I'll see you in the morning." The words were merely a whisper of sound, but brought Maggie momentarily to reality...a reality that had her breathing her lover in again, and appreciating him all over.

Eventually, she noticed only Shannon's body pressed against hers, and Maggie gradually realized that she and he were the sole occupants of the room. She wondered if he noticed this as well, because his head lifted from her neck briefly. However, blissfully, he returned, and she could feel his lips there, nestled in the hollow between her ear and collar bone.

She absorbed the sensations created by his mouth and his arms enveloping her, until he whispered against her delicate skin,

"Let's go upstairs, me love, so we can enjoy the las' bit o' time we ha' wi' each other."

Though his words were meant to move them toward the guest bedroom, the two held onto each other for a time, breathing in the scent and feel of the other. When he began to pull away from her, she held tight, pulling him closer to her body, confessing, "I'm not quite ready to let you go. These last days with you have been…" Maggie searched for an adequate word to articulate all of the emotions she had felt during their time together, but realized that no such word existed. Finally, she settled on "…heaven."

Though the word failed to encompass the spectrum of emotions she felt, it was all that she could come up with. If she were being honest with herself, she would also need to add "life-changing" as well as "future relationship-altering." She knew in that moment, as he held her snugly against his chest, she would never be the same, and no one or anything else would ever compare to the last several days of peaceful, emotional bliss she had experienced.

He then pulled away from her, but leaned in and kissed her deeply, if somewhat forcefully, on the mouth. Abruptly breaking away, Shannon looked into her eyes and agreed, "Ye're right, me love. If this is it, we bes' make the most of it." With that, he picked her up and cradled her against his chest, carrying her through the house and up the stairs.

Once in the bedroom, he laid her on the bed, following her down. He kissed her with a fervent passion, reveling in the taste and feel of her lips. His hands roamed, caressing her breasts and resting on her hips, until he had to see more of her. In one smooth motion, he ripped her shirt from her body, appreciating her swollen breasts. Wasting no time, he descended, taking one of her budding nipples into his mouth and suckling it in, teasing it with his swirling tongue.

Her responsive moan and gyrating hips expressed that she was more than open to his affections and he continued, pulling the pajama pants from her, so that she was fully exposed. Next, his face was buried in her bosom, as his hand twirled an enticing massage between her legs. His fingertips worked tirelessly to pleasure her, and he felt the hot wetness that was readying her for him.

He ascended to her mouth. Pulling her swollen lips into his mouth, he swirled her lips with his tongue, while teasing her intensely firing nerve endings with his wayward fingertips. Her breath caught in her throat, and she moved into him with her mouth and her hips.

"Oh Shannon," she muttered into the top of his head, as her hands made a trek of their own across his shoulders and upper back in an effort to remove his clothing. When she wasn't getting anywhere, she pushed on his chest, urging in a husky whisper, "I want to see more of you. Take it off."

He quickly obliged and they were both naked, skin to skin, and admiring the curves and valleys of each other's bodies. As her hands delved and explored, his did too, in a desperate perusal, as they knew it would be the last space of time they would occupy together.

"There's nothing better than you," he whispered into her neck, as he continued to feel her satiny soft skin. "Me love, I'll remember ye this way forever. I'll never forget ye, nor will I forget the way ye taste and feel under me skin." As he said this, his hands roamed nonstop over her body. He ended his exaltation by taking her nipple into his mouth and swirling the hardening bud with the tip of his tongue.

Maggie moaned, in a thrall from his ministrations, rubbing against him like a cat. After a moment, he pulled back, placing his hands on each hip, holding her still and studying her as if in an attempt to memorize every inch of her. She attempted to move, wanting to feel more of him, but his grip remained firm, and she looked into his eyes. The hunger she saw there stopped her movements and caused the moisture to pool deep between her thighs and her breath to leave her suddenly.

His lover suitably subdued, Shannon dove between her thighs, face first, and voraciously began devouring her, eliciting a hoarse and throaty moan. When his mouth began working her, his grip relaxed and her hips bucked involuntarily, affixing her more firmly to his mouth. Her hands automatically went to the top of his head, alternating pulling his hair and holding him more firmly to her.

His tongue danced and probed, sending delicious zings of sensation from where his mouth touched her, to the tips of her breasts. She delighted mindlessly in the intense pleasure as it grew into a monstrous storm that slowly and insidiously became too much for her to take.

Where she had been moving in a slow rhythmic dance, the thrust of Maggie's hips became more frantic; an erratic tango Shannon couldn't fail to notice. It must have been just as he wanted her, as he was driving her beyond the edge of control. With a last deep thrust of his tongue, he released his grip on her and raised himself over her, entering her and causing them both to cry out in tandem.

Maggie was already so close to the point of no return that she came instantly upon insertion. As he drove into her again and again, her post-cunnilingus pleasure was being revved up once more, as was his. She couldn't help but moan against his chest as it moved across her face. Her tongue whipped out, and she tasted the salt intermingled with his fluffy hairs there.

As he moved into her, rocking back and forth rhythmically with his hips, his chest stilled in response to feeling her mouth. She took advantage, swirling her tongue over the flattened disc of his nipple, causing it to stiffen and rise.

Responding to her touch, he initially slowed his pace in an effort to draw out the ecstasy for both of them. But the pressure must have become overwhelming, and he hurried to finish. As he sped up, faster and harder, he spent himself into her in one final powerful thrust before collapsing on top of her.

She held him to her breast, stroking the dampened top of his head, before moving to his back, continuously kneading and exploring. If this was the end of their time together, she wanted to commit as much of him to memory as she possibly could. With this in mind, she turned her face so that she could pull his essence into her body, inhaling deeply, in an effort to forever burn his scent into her memory and hold a piece of him in her forever.

His face toward her, he kissed her neck, pulling her scent into his lungs. His arms tensed and relaxed as she caressed his back. Gradually, his breathing slowed, becoming synchronous with hers.

As much as they wanted to cherish every moment, before either of them could help it, they both fell asleep.

Chapter Ten

When Maggie awakened, Shannon was gone, and she remembered suddenly that it was the day of her mother's funeral. Setting aside the thought of her lost lover, she jumped out of bed and moved toward the bathroom. Looking at the clock, she noted that it was 10:30. She had two hours before she needed to be at the funeral home to make final arrangements.

Hurriedly, Maggie took a quick shower, sending up a silent prayer for her hair to tame itself for the occasion. Drying off quickly, she ran her fingers through her hair in an attempt to pull the kinks out. Rolling her eyes, she decided that her mom probably would not begrudge her from heaven because her hair was unruly as usual.

After throwing on a small amount of make-up, she dressed in the black outfit she had chosen for the day. She gave her appearance a cursory glance before running out the door and then down the stairs.

To her relief, Morgan was waiting at the foot of the stairs, and John was at the front door, holding it ajar. Beyond him in the home's circle drive, there was a black limo. The be-tuxedoed chauffer, she could see, was standing next to the car with the back door open, waiting for them.

Seeing her surprised look, John explained, "I took the liberty of getting a car for the occasion. I hope you will find it satisfactory." Taken aback, Maggie had to clear her throat before answering, "Yes, thank you." The sentiment and effort brought tears to her eyes, and for the millionth time, she felt thankful for the friends in her life.

John, being ever the gentleman, gestured for her to precede him into the car. As she ducked into the backseat, with the assistance of the driver, she was followed closely by Morgan, and then John. Immediately, John went to work, pouring liquid out of bottles into glasses. Maggie wasn't sure what he was doing until he handed her one of the crystalline glasses. She looked down at it, puzzled. After a moment of her staring at the glass, John explained, "It's Jameson and cola; traditional for an Irish wake."

When she did not move to drink from it, but only stared at it contemplatively, he took the glass from her and replaced it with a drink that was the orange of sunset. "If that is too much, try this; it's refreshing, and you will likely enjoy it. It will…help you through your mother's wake."

Maggie accepted the glass that was thrust into her hand, taking a tentative sip. The citrusy, effervescent flavor exploded in her mouth, and she took a small gulp, enjoying the refreshing flavor. "I took the liberty of making mimosas for us," John explained, as he poured a drink for Morgan and himself. "It's not the traditional Irish Wake drink, but it will definitely take the edge off," he explained, as he took deep pulls from his own glass.

Maggie followed his example in an effort to numb her mind to the overwhelming emotions. Before they exited the neighborhood, she had drained her glass and John was pouring more for her. He must have sensed her need to drown her sorrows, ensuring that her cup continued running over, keeping a watchful eye on her glass as she worked to finish it.

When they pulled onto the turnpike, Morgan turned to Maggie and asked, "Are you expecting the she-witch today?" The question elicited a round of nervous giggles from Mag, as she realized that she wasn't, in fact, quite sure of who she expected would be present for her mother's funeral.

"I suspect," she began hesitantly, "that the she-witch will be quite hesitant to attend today." She took a deep swallow before continuing. "You know…since I put her in her place the last time I saw her." With that admission, she finished her drink while John promptly refilled her glass for her.

Morgan was silent for a moment as she processed the information, downing her glass as well. While John added juice and champagne for her, she smiled at Maggie. "Feels good, doesn't it?" The look in Maggie's eye as she nodded was fierce. The car was silent for the remainder of the drive.

Arriving at the funeral home, John picked up a large sealed container that had been hidden. When the chauffeur opened the door for him, John stepped out of the car, taking it with him. The chauffeur then moved to assist the two ladies in exiting, but John stood his ground, choosing to assist them himself.

Having already enjoyed several mimosas, Maggie was grateful for the steadying assistance. Morgan was out next, and as a group, the three walked in together.

Upon entering the funeral home, the first thing Maggie noticed was a familiar-looking red-haired man leaning against the wall opposite the door they had just come through. She had the strangest feeling that she had met him before and hesitated before being urged by Morgan to continue.

The small room where the body of Maggie's mother was placed for viewing had so many floral arrangements that their scent was apparent upon entry into the room. Having forgotten to order flowers, Maggie was stunned by the sight and the smell. This time when she stopped, she would not be prompted to move forward.

As she stared at the beautiful array of flowers, tears slid down her cheeks and she knew that she would remember the sight of her mother, surrounded by their beauty for all time. Morgan put her arm around Maggie's shoulder and whispered, "I knew you'd like it, and she deserved to have the flowers that she loved around her when you got to see her for the last time."

"Thank you so much, Morgan. This is a gift beyond measure to me."

Morgan hugged her friend and kissed her cheek, explaining, "It was John, actually. He has an account with Trochta's. I only told him what you like."

Maggie looked at John, pulled him in for a sturdy hug, and kissed him on the cheek. "Thank you so much, John! This is so special to me!"

He appeared taken aback by the sudden embrace, but nevertheless returned her affection, while looking helplessly over Maggie's head at Morgan. His expression said that the loving smile Morgan paid him was enough thanks, even if he was being held in a rib-cracking embrace.

When Maggie finally let go of John, she wiped her eyes, and the trio walked toward the casket. Maggie admired her mother's make-up; she looked so peaceful. After staring down at her mom for several moments, she turned around, ready to join Morgan and John.

To her surprise, the familiar looking red-haired man she had noticed earlier was sitting near the back of the room, staring at her. In a daze, she stared back until Morgan noticed and turned to see what had captured her attention. John had been whispering to her, but when he noticed Morgan's distraction, he also turned to study the man at the back of the room.

As if summoned by their watchfulness, the man stood to his full height and slowly approached the trio. John's body reflexively stiffened, and he leaned toward the ladies in preparation for any adversity the newcomer might bring.

The man cleared his throat and then, looking at Maggie, asked, "Are ye Maggie?" His voice sounded strange, as though he was exercising great control in talking to her.

Maggie blinked, nodded, and belatedly realized that he had the same accent she had been hearing from Shannon and his friends for the last several days.

The man looked closely at her for a long time, as if trying to decide something. Finally, he kneeled in front of her, and took her hand, sandwiching it between his. John was poised as if ready to pounce on him but remained still, as if attempting to determine the man's motives.

Maggie looked into the man's eyes and was startled to see tears there. She wondered how he could be so upset about her mother's death when he surely had not known her; for if he had, she would've already been acquainted with him.

The words that came out of his mouth caused her heart to jump into her throat, where it pounded nearly as fiercely as when she had awakened a week earlier to her mother's death-glazed eyes.

"I never ha' met ye, dear; tis wha' she wanted, an' I canna say as I blame 'er for it. But ye're me wee one, Maggie." He stared into her eyes, begging her silently to understand everything that was in his words, as well as the things he wasn't saying.

Maggie stood frozen in silence as she and the stranger held each other's awed gaze. Finally, she stammered, "What?" which was the only thing she could manage to say.

He swallowed audibly before continuing his explanation, "Ye're ma and I...we fell in love wi' each other, but ye're ma's ma didna like me in the slightest." He looked around at the mention of her grandmother, as if uttering her name might conjure up her presence.

"But why..." Maggie started, having difficulty completing a sentence. As she struggled to form a coherent thought, he stood back up to his full height of six foot two, stopping her garbled words, and handed her a slip of paper. "I'm stayin' in town fer the next while, lass. I donut wish ter interrupt ye're dear ma's funeral fer ye, but if ye'd like to hear me explanation, please come see me."

As quickly as he had disrupted her life, he was gone, and Maggie was left clutching the scant link to the man who claimed to be her biological father. As she turned and stared blankly at her mother's lifeless body, silent tears began to fall.

John placed a full glass of mimosa in her hand. She drank in a long succession of swallows, and he quickly refilled it for her.

****

Jordan awakened in a fog. Noting the time, she slowly realized she had slept for nearly twenty-four hours. Remembering her ordeal, she was thankful for that time and desperately wanted to return to the peaceful oblivion of sleep; however, she knew she needed to go to work.

Feeling around for her phone, she checked her texts and saw that Sam had messaged her: *Don't know what's happened, girl, but the 411 is that they're firing you. Have they called you? You should come in and talk to Miss Joan ASAP. Do you need me to pick you up for work today?*

Glancing at the time again, she realized she was scheduled to be at work in less than an hour. Although her head was spinning, she struggled to move off of the bed. Her bladder was full, so it would be the first thing she addressed. Grabbing her phone, she moved toward the restroom.

Looking at her call log, she saw that she had several voicemails. The first was from work. As she began to pee, the relief was so intense that she had goosebumps. However, the dread from listening to the voicemail from her manager overshadowed any joy she had in the emptying of her overstretched bladder. With her cell on speaker, she listened to Mary's hateful voice. "I don't know what you done to piss people off, girly girl, but you need to come in right away and have a meeting with Dr. Peters and me. You're suspended until that meeting takes place. I'm not sure exactly what it's about." There was a strange sound, but then Jordan heard the barely audible words "sexual harassment," before the message ended.

Her head already cloudy from her drug-induced drowsiness did not help the feeling of trepidation that was beginning to fill her chest. She again wished for nothing more than to sleep forever.

The tears began streaming down her face as if a dam had broken. It seemed fitting, as it was in direct proportion to the hopelessness she felt at her situation. Thinking of behavior that could be deemed sexual harassment brought her thoughts to Dr. Schambaugh and what had transpired between them in the medicine room. Somewhere in her brain, a thought flickered, but was as fleeting as catching air with her fingers.

After she shuffled out of the bathroom, she laid on her bed and stared at the ceiling, trying to figure out what to do and what could have happened to her. She was almost certain she had been raped; the tissue outside and inside of her vagina was extremely tender and had bled a little, although she could have sworn she remembered the nurse saying there was no injury there. And the bruises: there were several around her inner thighs and her wrists. She couldn't explain them any other way.

Giving in to her sinking despair, Jordan reached across her bed and scooped up the rest of the pills that had spilled on the bedside table. A large handful, which she didn't bother to count. In that moment, she made a snap decision. Tossing them all into her mouth, she took several large gulps of water, and rested her head on her pillow, eyes closed as she awaited infinite slumber to overtake her.

****

By the time the funeral was over, Maggie was well on her way to being intoxicated, which she decided was no small mercy. It had been a small service, consisting of her brother and one of her cousins, along with the trio that she made up with Morgan and John. Maggie wasn't surprised, nor disappointed. Her mom had been a shut-in long before her illness required her to be, and they had never had a large or close family. Even her brother had spent most of his post-adolescent life with his father and had never been particularly close to their mother.

As the group filed into the limo after rounds of hugs were given, John turned to Mag and asked, "Where would you like to go? I'm leaving it up to you."

Maggie stared out the window, considering his question. If she was honest with herself, what she really wanted was to be in bed, with Shannon buried deep inside of her. She could still smell him on her skin, even though she had showered. Closing her eyes for a moment had her picturing him, which caused a pleasurable shiver to move through her.

Finally, she turned to John and answered. "I could use a stiff drink. Wanna go to a bar with me?" John smiled at her in response, instructing the driver on where to take them.

Chapter Eleven

The following morning, Maggie awakened to a room full of blinding sunlight and an equally blinding headache. Her throat felt as though it were full of sand, and when she tilted her head to the side, the room began spinning as though she were on a tilt-o-whirl. She had to grip the sheets to gain any semblance of stillness.

At that moment, Maggie felt someone moving next to her in the bed, and she searched her brain to try and figure out who it might be. She slowly turned her head and saw the top of Morgan's dark head. As much as her hangover made her hurt everywhere, she couldn't help but smile. Her best friend would never leave her in her most difficult moment.

Sensing movement, Morgan opened her eyes and looked over at Maggie. "Hi there! You're alive! I'm quite relieved for that little miracle!"

Upon closer inspection, Maggie realized that she and Morgan were not the only two in the bed. Following her gaze, Morgan explained, "It's John. I was worried about you, and he was worried about me." After looking over at him, she smiled brightly and told Maggie, "He wanted to sleep on the floor; said he thought you'd be more comfortable that way. But I wouldn't hear of it. I hope you don't mind."

Maggie smiled warmly at the thought of sleeping with her best friend and her boyfriend. When Morgan inquired about her grin, she answered, "I hadn't been laid in years, and now, just as soon as my mom passes, I've slept with more people in a week than I have in years." This elicited a round of giggles from the two women, which startled John, and had him pulling Morgan more firmly into his body. As Maggie admired their intimacy, the dull ache returned to her chest, and she fought to swallow the lump that was rising in her throat.

The peacefulness of the room was interrupted when Morgan received a text message and reached for her phone. "My kids are back!" she exclaimed excitedly as she read it. As if she had announced the start of a race, she and John climbed out of the bed and rushed to the door, leaving Maggie alone. Groaning, she pulled a pillow over her head as she turned over and let her overwhelming exhaustion lull her back to sleep.

****

With the funeral over and the need to return to work looming, Maggie found herself in a troubling and difficult transition back to everyday life. She felt as though something was left undone. There was a tremendous feeling of some lack of completion of which she could not pinpoint the source, and as she arrived home for the first time in nearly a week, she racked her brain, trying to figure it out.

Upon entering the small home she had shared with her mother for many years, she couldn't help but see her everywhere she turned. Not surprisingly, the tears began, and she felt that she needed to leave or else she was sure she would be so overcome with grief that she would never escape.

Turning around, she ran out of the house to her car and sped away as though being pursued by a madman. When she made it to the first stoplight, she had a sudden impulse to get answers. Pulling out the slip of paper that the red-haired man had given to her the day before, she dialed the number.

Ten minutes later, she was in front of the hotel where her biological father was staying – that is, if she believed him, which she hadn't yet decided. With shaky hands, she knocked on his door and waited on trembling legs.

When he answered the door, Maggie was taken aback. Behind him stood a beautiful brunette who did not appear to be much older than Maggie herself. He held the door so that it opened wide for her to enter, and she slowly stepped inside.

Once the door closed behind her, she felt slightly dizzy and made her way to the bed nearest to the door. After sitting down, she looked around, not knowing what to expect from the two in the room.

The woman watched her for a moment without speaking. The red-haired man approached her and looked as though he would hug her, but then lowered his arms, as if he thought better of it, holding out his hand for her to shake.

"Seamus," he told her. She grasped his hand for a moment, staring at it dumbly, until she realized that he was giving her his name, along with his hand.

Eventually she nodded in acknowledgement, and he sat down on the opposite bed, followed shortly by the woman, who sat on his left. She was the next to speak. Offering her hand, she announced, "It's nice to meet ye, Maggie. I'm Fiona, *teaghlach* of ye're da's."

Maggie weakly shook the hand that was offered to her, swallowing in an attempt to clear her throat, and process the title the woman had given to her. She looked from one to the other of them, wide-eyed, and shook her head to clear it. Lightheaded again, she was having a difficult time processing everything.

Fortunately, she was spared from having to make coherent words when he offered, "Ye're prolly wondeerin' why I contacted ye now, after all these years." His own eyes were wide open as he watched her, as though he was taking in every detail of her appearance.

Nervously, he cleared his throat and continued. "As I was sayin' yesterday, ye're ma and I fell in love all dem years ago, and what came of it was you. But ye're gran' didna like me, and one night when I was way sloshed from the whiskey, ye're ma was taken away when ye're gran came an' fetched 'er."

He continued to stare at his daughter expectantly. Maggie felt as if he was awaiting her condemnation or, in some way, that he needed her forgiveness in order to be absolved. She remained silent, taking in his explanation and processing it. Finally, she verbalized the question that had preyed on her mind her entire life. "How long have you known about me?"

He closed his eyes and sighed, as though the answer was the hardest thing he would ever disclose. After several moments of silence, he leaned forward and revealed, "I've known about ye all ye're life, Maggie." He then opened his mouth and then closed it, as if trying to form a coherent explanation. Maggie continued to stare at him while he stumbled over the words that he obviously found so difficult to express.

"Ye're ma called me not long after she was taken away. I ha' been worried sick over her for weeks, not knowin' was she hurt, or run off, or what." He paused, looking conflicted, and then persevered, "When she finally called 'twas to say that she was wi' child, but also that she didna wan' me to try an' pursue her. She said tha' her ma wouldna like her to ha' anythin' to do wi' me, an' she said her ma had another man picked out fer 'er."

Maggie could easily imagine her grandmother pulling off that type of manipulation with her mother, and even more so if her mother had been happy. The old bat had never been satisfied until everyone around her was as miserable as she. And the man Maggie's mother had married, who was her brother, Pete's father, had never loved her or her mother. He had married her for the money that her grandmother had promised him. And while he had abused Maggie's mother, he merely tolerated Maggie, ignoring her for the most part.

Unfortunately, it wasn't until he had gotten his son that he finally had decided that he wanted no more to do with Maggie or her mother. Maggie was seven when he left, taking her baby brother with him. From then on, Maggie only saw Pete during summers when they would both stay with their grandmother.

Seamus cleared his throat, bringing her back to the present. She blinked to clear her vision and nodded in understanding. "That woman could manipulate a priest into an affair with a prostitute," she conceded.

The corner of Seamus's mouth twitched, and Maggie thought that he was stifling a smile. "Tha' she could, lass," he agreed before amending, "not meaning any disrespect, of course."

She waved his comment away, asking, "You got anything to drink around here?"

The other woman- Fiona- stood, walking around the bed before pulling a bottle of scotch from under the bathroom sink. "How do ye take it, dearie?"

Maggie replied, "Straight up with ice, please."

When she brought her the drink, Maggie quickly downed it and briefly squirmed around on the bed, trying to get more comfortable. Once she was settled in, she began talking. "My grandmother is an awful person. I can see her doing such an unthinkable thing to my mother. How did the two of you meet?"

Seamus seemed to let his breath out, and Maggie was surprised to realize that he had been holding it. Finally, he began, "'Twas when ye're ma came to Dublin fer a trip during school." His eyes lit up as he recalled, "She was the mos' beautiful creature I ha' ever laid eyes on, and I couldna keep my eyes off her when I firs' saw 'er."

Fiona smirked, and when he looked over at her inquiringly, she added, "Ye're hands either, as I've heard told."

His face turned beet red at the remark, and he gave a subtle nod that was accentuated with a contemplative, "aye." Maggie wondered if her mother's and father's passion had been anything like what she and Shannon had experienced with each other.

"How long were you two together before grandma made her come back?" Maggie's curiosity was becoming more heightened by the moment. Her mother had never spoken of her father, and every time she'd asked, her mother had seemed saddened by the question and would withdraw into herself for days. Eventually, Maggie had stopped asking altogether.

Seamus cleared his throat and told her, "She would ha' left after only a week, but instead she stayed wi' me fer a blissful three months o' heaven. I ha' never gotten over losin' her in all these years."

Maggie stood up and walked to the sink, where the whiskey was being chilled in a bucket of ice, trying to dispel some of her mounting nervousness. She needed more booze as much as she needed to move around and mull over everything Seamus had disclosed.

Seeing the two- her relatives- on the bed in the mirror, Maggie saw them talking quietly. Listening intently, it occurred to her that they weren't speaking English. As she watched them interacting, she wondered about the circumstances of their relationship, and trying to recall what it was that the woman had called her father. They were clearly quite familiar with each other, although she didn't think they were together intimately.

As if in answer to her unspoken question, Fiona stepped up to her and said, "Ye're me *teaghlach*, dear." Seeing Maggie's confusion, she provided, "I think in English it's called 'family.' In fact, ye're *col ceathrar* also."

Maggie shook her head in confusion and Fiona turned to look at Seamus, as if seeking assistance in the translation. "Cousin," Seamus provided. "Fiona is me brother's daughter, though she is much like a daughter to me, as much as she ha' been with me since her da' passed."

Fiona looked back at Maggie, who was becoming excited at the idea of having a cousin. Maggie's family had always kept away from she and her mother, and she had always felt a sense of loss, although she thought it was rather tacky of them to stay away simply because of her grandmother's rude insistence.

"Cousin!" Maggie exclaimed as an overlarge smile plastered itself to her face. Her arms wrapped around Fiona, almost as if of their own volition. Although seeming to be taken aback, her cousin's arms returned the embrace.

Suddenly, Maggie began to feel lightheaded again, and took another drink in an attempt to stop it. Fiona took a drink from her own cup, and they looked at each other in awkward silence for a moment.

"Ye two don' need ter be scairt of each other now that ye ha' fount each other." This prompted grins from the two women.

Seamus added, "Come to think of, ye have a great many cousins in fact that ye've never met back at home."

Upon hearing this news, Maggie's head turned toward him and her heart fluttered, so that she had to take a seat on the bed, or she feared she would fall. In fact, the room began to spin and she was having difficulty drawing in breath effectively. Naturally, she leaned her head forward so that it was between her knees, and sucked in air.

Seamus sat next to her and lightly massaged the back of her neck. "There there. Take it easy. Breathe," he soothed in a soft and quiet voice.

When she was finally able to regulate her breathing, she sat up, holding her head in her hands. "I have a family?" she said in a combination of both disbelief and statement, stunned at the revelation.

The room was silent as Fiona and Seamus watched Maggie absorb the news. Finally, she exclaimed, "I have a family!" and the three were all smiles, for similar, but different reasons.

After the joyous chuckling subsided, Seamus asked his daughter shyly, "So ye believe me then, lass?"

Maggie thought about it for a few seconds and nodded. Somehow, she felt strongly that he was indeed being truthful with her. She hoped it wasn't merely the excitement and anticipation of having a family that goaded her into the belief.

Seamus teared up, seeming relieved, and took her into his arms. Pulling her into his lap, he hugged her against his chest like a little girl. She allowed him to hold her, and she imagined for a moment that his comforting embrace is what it would have been like for her as a small child with pain or heartache, had he been part of her life all of those years ago.

Finally, he let her go and she sat down on the bed next to him. The three spent the rest of the evening talking and becoming acquainted with each other.

****

When Samantha King awakened, she called her work wife to check on her. *Scratch that,* she thought, remembering that Jordan had more than likely been canned. The thought infuriated her, and for the thousandth time in the last several days, she considered quitting the job where she had worked for the last five years.

After the eighth ring, the phone went to voicemail, and Sam decided she needed to go check on her friend again. She had knocked on the door the evening before, but had received no answer. Figuring that she was asleep, Sam had left, but couldn't escape the nagging feeling in the back of her mind. The fact that she was still unable to contact her friend gave her a sense of urgency, and her heart began pounding in her chest.

When she arrived at Jordan's door, she knocked loudly while simultaneously ringing the doorbell. When no sound came from the other side of the door, she knocked harder, attempting to turn the handle. It was locked, so she banged, and then yelled through the door, "Jordan! Are you there?"

As she stepped back, trying to decide what to do, she realized that she had an audience. Fortunately, one of the spectators who had gathered was one that Sam recognized as the apartment manager. Approaching him, she explained, "I think my friend is hurt in there. I need you to unlock the door while I call an ambulance."

Sam was surprised by her own words. She wasn't sure which was more startling: that she had blurted it out, or that she was so sure that it was true. But she pulled out her phone and dialed 911.

Luckily, the manager carried the keys on him, and he retrieved a large, full set from his back belt loop. As Sam entered the apartment, the dispatcher answered. When she saw her friend drooling and discovered that she was unresponsive, she was unable to speak, handing the phone to the manager.

"Jordan!" Sam cried into her friend's face as she shook her. Lifting one of Jordan's eyelids, Sam could feel the blood drain from her face as she saw that the pupil was fixed and dilated. Remembering from work, seeing a patient code and the way the nurse had responded, Sam rubbed her knuckles roughly over Jordan's chest as she shouted in her ear.

To Sam's relief, it resulted in a brief reaction, and Jordan became combative, attempting to push her hands away. Sam was further relieved when she could faintly hear the ambulance approaching.

She placed her hand over the pulse in Jordan's neck and noted that it was dangerously slow. Looking over at the table on the opposite side of the bed, she noticed an empty prescription bottle laying on its side. Reaching across the bed, she grabbed the bottle and saw that it was Valium. Next to Jordan's head, four small, round pills were nestled in the folds of the sheet, giving Sam a sinking feeling.

Finally, Sam could hear a commotion outside of the apartment, and a stretcher appeared in the living room, flanked by a paramedic. He rushed into the bedroom and went straight to work. Sam backed out of the way and watched in numb shock as he worked to save Jordan's life.

After what seemed like an eternity, Jordan was strapped onto the stretcher and quickly wheeled out of the apartment to the waiting ambulance. Sam wasn't sure if she would be allowed to accompany her, but decided she wasn't going to wait for permission. Before the medic closed the door, she jumped in and seated herself next to her friend.

At the hospital, Sam was not allowed into the trauma bay with Jordan, instead being sent into a family room. Coincidentally, they were at the same hospital they had come to just a few days before for the SANE exam, and Sam found herself in the same room in which Jordan had encountered the bastard cop.

Fear for her friend as well as anger at the injustice that had been served had Sam so frustrated and furious that she wanted to punch something. She had begun pacing when the door swung open, and she saw that it was the nurse practitioner from the SANE exam.

"I'm sorry to meet again under such tragic circumstances," she started, as she closed the door behind her. Sam had a sinking feeling, but as the NP sat down, she took the chair next to her. As the lady began speaking to Sam, she immediately felt more comfortable, despite the circumstances.

"The patient and you…how are you related?" the nurse practitioner inquired. Sam had worked in healthcare long enough to know where the line of questioning was headed, and lied easily, stating that she was Jordan's sister.

The nurse practitioner nodded briefly in acknowledgment, and then began discussing Jordan's prognosis with her. "Your sister is in critical condition, Sam." Impressed that she remembered her name, she decided that she liked the la- Annie- and appreciated her candor. "The toxicology screen has not come back yet, but the medic said she was found with a nearly empty bottle of Valium?"

Sam was thankful that the information had been passed on and confirmed, "Yes. I think it was the medication you prescribed her; so it must have been however many you gave her, minus a few pills that I found next to her on the bed."

Annie's swift intake of breath told Sam quite a bit about how poorly her friend was doing, and she received further confirmation when Annie stated, "I don't believe in beating around the bush, and I'm going to give you the news straight. Your sister is in a fight for her life and it's very touch-and-go right now."

Annie was silent for a few moments, allowing Sam to absorb the news, but eventually informed her, "The team has admitted her to the ICU. You can go see her in about an hour, after they get her settled in."

Sam processed the information and racked her brain, trying to think of what questions to ask. Her healthcare experience told her that Annie was likely to be the best source for intel about Jordan's condition.

She remained seated next to the NP for several minutes, trying to tease out an intelligent question. Annie seemed to sense her struggle, and answered some of the unasked questions that were fighting for purchase in her brain. "I imagine this is a difficult situation for you, and I am sorry to say that there is not much I can tell you at this point. Like I said, it is really touch-and-go right now and she is going to have to fight through this. We have the best treatment that technology has to offer, and we are supporting her as much as we possibly can. The rest is up to her."

Sam let out the breath she had been holding and despite the difficult news, felt at ease from what she had just been told. "Thank you very much," she told the NP. She knew her relief must be palpable, since Annie smiled slightly, and gave a small nod that was nearly imperceptible.

After standing to go, she turned to Sam, telling her, "You're welcome to wait in here, or you can go on up to the sixth floor if you'd like. If you go up, just sit in the waiting room for a bit. In an hour it'll be one o'clock. If they've not updated you by then, just go to the nurse's station and ask if you can go in and see her."

Sam had also stood and was preparing to leave when Annie stopped her and advised, "They do get busy up there. If you go longer than an hour without an update, gentle reminders are sometimes helpful."

Sam thanked her and then exited the ER, anxious to get to the sixth floor and await news, as well as call work and notify them that she would not be there for her shift. The rest of the day was filled with apprehension as she awaited news of Jordan's condition.

Chapter Twelve

On Saturday, Maggie spent the day becoming acquainted with her father and cousin as they were getting to know the city, with Maggie acting as their tour guide. The weather had suddenly changed, as was typical in Oklahoma: by mid-afternoon, the snow was all but melted and the temperature had warmed into the forties. While they were in Maggie's car, the sun became a bit too much but when they walked outside, the wind gusts made it more comfortable to wear a sweater.

Seamus noted the contrast with indignation. "Mmmph! How ye Americans can go wi' 'out bein' sick all the time is beyond me." Maggie laughed as they walked into Penn Square Mall, recalling some of the patients she had cared for over the years; in particular, those who had initially become sick with garden-variety seasonal allergies, but had eventually been hospitalized due to exacerbation of the resulting illness that sometimes came about from chronic sniffles and dampened mucous membranes.

"Well, sometimes we don't," Maggie admitted. "It's called seasonal allergies, and it's much worse when the weather changes constantly."

The three walked together quietly until they arrived at the movie theatre. As they entered, Maggie smiled to herself, considering the enjoyable time she was having with her newfound family. She dreaded her return to work, which was set to happen in two days' time. She just wasn't sure she was ready for it, and further, she didn't want to miss any time with her father or cousin.

The thought brought back the feeling of the acute losses over the last several days, and Maggie could feel a knot of grief gathering in her stomach and constricting her throat. She was thankful for the darkened theatre, and casually swiped at the tears that slid down her cheeks. Luckily, they had chosen a comedy. She needed a distraction from her sorrow, even if it was only temporary.

Later, Maggie took them to one of her favorite restaurants. As the three of them enjoyed a giant pizza, Seamus asked, "So where did ye live wi' ye're ma, Maggie?" She was confused, as she didn't recall telling him that she had lived with her mother. But the previous evening, she had been pretty drunk, so she figured that she very well could have poured out her entire life story without remembering.

"Not too far from here, actually," Maggie replied. She noticed that Seamus's eyes lit up after she said it, and decided that he was likely interested in seeing the house that she had shared with her mother. As she pondered the idea, her heart actually lightened. To be able to share her mother's memory and essence with someone who had known her, and who loved her as much, if not more than she, gave her no small measure of joy and relief.

"Would you like to see it?" she asked. Though his face gave nothing away, she thought that his eyes widened at the invitation. However, he merely nodded slightly, finishing his scotch.

The rest of the meal was finished in contemplative, but not awkward silence, before the trio made their way to Maggie's car. With the sun having set, the temperature had dropped noticeably and the sweaters from earlier were no longer sufficient to block the chill. This time in the car, Seamus said nothing of the weather, as he intensely focused at the road before them. Maggie wondered if he was as nervous as she.

By the time they approached the driveway, Maggie had a white-knuckled grip on the steering wheel. She wasn't sure if it was her attempt at maintaining a grip despite her sweaty palms, or the effort she was having to exert to keep the car under control through the intermittent patches of ice. When they came to a stop, no one moved or breathed for a moment, as though they were of one anxious mind, cautious about what might happen next.

Finally, Maggie shut off the engine, and the air quickly became too frigid to comfortably remain in the car. "We'el, shall we?" Fiona asked, ending the shattering silence. With this, they opened their doors in unison.

Once inside, Maggie looked around, appraising her home as if seeing it for the first time. The living room was cluttered, with her mother's adjustable bed stuffed in the corner, and the rest of the furniture crowded around it. She paused just inside the threshold for a moment, hesitant to let anyone else in. It almost felt like a betrayal to her mother to bring strangers into the personal space she had inhabited for so long.

Shaking her head at the thought, she stepped aside and allowed the two behind her to enter. Seamus walked inside first, and as though with an otherworldly instinct, he moved to her mother's bed, caressing the pillow as if he could still feel her presence there.

He sucked in an audible breath, exclaiming, "I can still smell 'er here." Maggie could see the shadows in his eyes as the tears began. Fiona hurried to his side, pulling him in for a hug. Maggie had to sit down. A separate part of her brain that was rational noted that the place where she had so roughly plopped down was the same exact spot from where she had watched the medics work on her mother the week before.

After a few minutes of the two embracing each other, Seamus pulled away from Fiona and looked down at the bed. He again stroked the pillow, asking Maggie, "Would ye mind if I laid down here, Maggie?"

It took her a few breaths to realize he was speaking to her. Snapping out of her fog, she nodded, then stood and went into the kitchen to retrieve a bottle of vodka. Reseating herself on the couch, she opened the clear bottle and took a deep whiff, staring into it. After careful consideration, she took a swig straight from the container as she observed Seamus's supine form, stretched out on her mother's bed with the pillow over his face.

Fiona stood over him for a short time before turning toward Maggie. Eventually, she walked across the room and joined her on the couch. "Can I share a drink with ya?" she asked.

Startled out of her reverie, Maggie looked over at her cousin and handed the bottle to her. After taking a drink, Fiona's face screwed up and she remarked, "Mmmph! I thought fer sure it'd be like drinkin' the hooch me mum used to buy, but it's no like that."

"Was it vodka?" Maggie asked, curious about the types of things that went on, and the drinks people enjoyed, in Ireland. This brought Shannon's face to the forefront of her thoughts and she suddenly felt the profound sadness that she had managed to keep hidden since her second encounter with her father.

"Mmmm, aye. That it 'twas. But none so stout as this lot, and we Irish like ter drink, aye?" Maggie nodded, considering that she was, in fact, at least half Irish, and enjoyed tying one on quite a lot.

The two sat together in companionable silence, taking turns sipping from the bottle. Finally, Maggie turned to her cousin and inquired, "Do you have any brothers or sisters, Fiona?"

Before answering, Fiona took a large swallow from the bottle and sighed deeply. "Aye. I have a few of 'em, though we donut see much o' each other."

Fiona was quiet for so long that Maggie thought she would discuss her siblings no longer, but finally she continued, "Ye see, me mum an' I donut get on well much. Tha's why ye're da took me on ter raise. Me mum didna want me much after me da passed. I was wee then. Mmmm, must ha' been about three."

After she said this to Maggie, Fiona closed her eyes and took another long drag from the bottle. Maggie saw a shudder go through her. Fiona's situation reminded her of her own, where the estrangement from her grandmother bled into her relationship with the rest of her family.

She was organizing her thoughts in an attempt to assemble all of the questions she wanted ask, but was interrupted by Fiona stating, as if to the room, "It 'twas the drink tha' made her so mean; at least it's wha' I tell meself. Other ways it makes no sense fer a grown woman to be jealous o' a wee babby. But me da always rained attention on me before he passed, an' she didna like it much. I remember her pinchin' me an' the like when I was wi' her when me da wasna there."

Maggie had taken possession of the bottle during Fiona's soliloquy, and she took a gulp before confiding in her cousin, "My grandma was the same way. I always hated spending summers with her, other than the fact that I got to see my brother then. But that old woman was awful. Sometimes she would lock us in the closet, or she'd cut my hair short and ugly out of spite."

Fiona gasped at this revelation. Maggie thought it was due to shock or pity at what she had disclosed, but surprisingly Fiona asked, "Is ye're gramma and me ma the same woman?" stunning Maggie with the question.

Fiona continued, explaining, "Ye're da would send me to stay wit' me ma sometimes during holiday or school break ter give me some time wit' me *teaghlach*, though not me ma. I s'pose he always knew she wasna nice to me. I canna say it 'twas no worth it though. It gave me time wi' me *dearthair's* an' *dearfuir's*."

Maggie surmised that the last words were specific members of her family, and it was confirmed when Seamus emerged from beneath a sea of blankets, speaking quietly to them. "I'm glad ter hear tha' ye think it 'twas worth it, love, and I reckon ye're brothers and sisters were more than glad ye were there to care fer them when ye're ma was too *berco* ter be carin' fer 'em proper. But I am sorry tha' she was sae a cat ter ya. I ken she was nay a saint, but I didna know she was tha' bad wit' it, lass. Fer tha' I do apologize to ye, even though it falls woefully short o' what ye deserve fer it."

His voice thickened towards the end of his statement, and Maggie thought that he was working to choke back some of his emotions. When she looked sideways at Fiona, she saw the raw emotion on her face. Maggie wondered if she might be angry at her uncle, but with the next statement she realized she had misinterpreted the reason behind her expression.

"Donut dare ter blame ye're self fer the actions of tha' woman, Uncail." The fierceness with which she addressed her uncle was somewhat shocking, following the soft spoken words, and Maggie flinched. "Ye did more fer me than most would, an' a right good job ye did wit' me too. Mos' wouldna care so much fer a babe tha' was no theirs, even if they was their kin. I would no hear ye speak ill of ye're self fer wha' someone else did. Tha' wench will be judged one day when she faces her maker, an' ye will as well. I wager ye'll be rewarded fer the care and sacrifice ye ha' given on me behalf."

Maggie's rational mind had her noticing that her cousin crossed herself when she spoke of God, and wondered if she was Catholic- as she had learned from Shannon- that a good many other Irish were. However, a larger part of her mind had her considering what she had just learned about her father; that he had taken on such an enormous responsibility for so long spoke volumes about the kind of man he was, and gave Maggie a much more favorable opinion of his character than she previously had.

Fiona was breathing heavily after her tirade, but was not quite finished expressing herself. It appeared as though she was going to continue until Seamus interrupted her, stating, "Donut worry ye're self about me, ya dear sweet girl. Ye mean more to me than wha' any other can say about me or you, and I donut take to heart any such ramblings; and ye shouldna either."

"Uncail, ye can say donut worry ye're self abou' me, but donut fool ye're self. I will accept the criticism aboot ye from no one. Wha' I am meanin' to say, is if'n someone is bad mouthin' ye, I willna stand fer it. Ye cared fer me an' ye are mine. I willna ha' anyone doubtin' ye or ye're intentions. I willna stan' by idly while it happens."

The room was quiet as they all processed Fiona's emotionally-driven speech. Maggie thought her cousin's words were spoken as much to defend Seamus as to describe his character to her. When she glanced over at him, she saw him differently than she had at first. This time, the natural arrogance in the stamp of his face that she had noticed before looked more tired and sad.

Maggie's heart went out to him, and to herself, for the time and closeness that had been lost due to her grandmother's heartless manipulations. She also thought of her mother and the longing she must have had throughout Maggie's life. She could recall times when her mother would stare at her as though seeing someone else, and recognized how terribly difficult it must have been for her.

Before she could think more on it, Maggie made a snap decision, crossing the room and sitting down by her father's side. Brushing back the hair that hid his face exposed the tears that had fallen, and Maggie gently assured him, "Do not be sad for me,

father, and do not think that I blame you for being away from me."
He looked into her eyes as she spoke the words to him, and Maggie
could see that he was having difficulty believing that his daughter
would forgive him for his absences.

"Eh? How could ye not blame me fer being away from ye
ye're whole life, *mo inion*; me daughter." His voice broke as he
asked, and Maggie could plainly see that he was trying his best to
keep the tears at bay.

"Because I don't blame you; I blame my wretched
grandmother for scheming the way she has. And besides, I had a
good life with my mother." She worked to form the next words, and
then finally stated, "It's her that I pity more than anyone in all of
this. To be made to stay away from one that you so deeply love...to
live a half-life, and then waste away, only to die alone."

As Maggie took in her father lying in the same place her
mother had once lain for endless hours, the irony of the situation
struck her suddenly, and she laughed. Strangely, it was not a small
chuckle; it was a long, heart-filled guffaw. Seamus looked at her,
alarmed, as though he thought she had lost her mind. When her
merriment subsided, she explained, "It's funny, but in an ironic sort
of way. You're lying here in exactly the same spot my mom laid for
so long. It's a shame that you have missed each other by merely a
handful of days."

As she finished, the tears began falling, and she felt a
profound sadness, as all of the emotions from the last several
days came crashing in on her at once. Before she knew it she
was scooped up and cradled onto Seamus's lap. He gently rocked
her as she wept, and quietly said things to her that she couldn't
understand, but which soothed her nonetheless. After several
minutes, she felt a hand smoothing her hair back, and realized that
it was Fiona's. The racking sobs continued, until she eventually

cried them out. She was sure there were no more tears in her body, as she felt completely drained.

Some time later- Maggie was uncertain if it was minutes or hours- she was put to bed, Fiona lying beside her. The two snuggled together through the night, and Maggie couldn't help but be reminded of Morgan and the way that she had cared for her. Though she felt sorrow over her recent losses, she also felt an unfamiliar completeness for the first time in a very long while.

Chapter Thirteen

The next week was difficult for Maggie as she returned to work. Randomly, she would break down and need to run to the ladies' room. She didn't want to be pitied by her co-workers or patients. She simply wanted to work and get through the day and night.

Maggie ran into Dr. Schambaugh on Wednesday, her third day back at work. He asked her if she was looking forward to their date on Friday, and she answered that she was. Surprisingly it was true. Not as much that she wanted to be with him, but for a desperately-needed distraction. She had been obsessing over Shannon lately, thinking she saw him in random places: once at a grocery store, and twice in a vehicle behind her while stopped at a traffic light. While her father and cousin had remained at her home for the last several days, keeping her happy and her mind occupied, she couldn't help but think of Shannon and the time they had spent together.

Thursday was Maggie's first day off, and she decided to cook for her family. Knowing they would be leaving the following Sunday made her want to do all that she could to make the most of their remaining time. Had it not been for her need to replace Shannon's loss, she would've cancelled her date with David.

As she contemplated dinner ideas, she eventually decided on one of her favorites: homemade chili with cheese and Fritos. She had no idea whether they ate Frito chili pie in Ireland, but was excited to introduce it to them if not. Additionally, the weather had changed yet again- this time to a winter storm- and she decided that this would be the perfect meal to warm them.

While cooking, she was joined in the kitchen by her father and cousin, and was delighted when her father began singing Irish ballads. The two women giggled together when his voice cracked, which only encouraged him further.

By the time the meal was ready, the three had drank quite a bit. Not much of the chili ended up being eaten, but it was nonetheless enthusiastically enjoyed by her family. After the trio cleaned the kitchen, Maggie taught them to play Mexican Train, her favorite domino game.

As the night wore on, they became progressively drunker and increasingly louder. Before they knew it, it was five in the morning, and Seamus was falling asleep in his drink. "Come on now, Uncail, let's get ye in bed," Fiona told him, as she struggled to get him to his feet.

Maggie stepped over to his other side, and both women labored to drag him over to the bed. After plopping him onto the mattress, they covered him up.

"Do ye want me to sleep wit' ye again tonight, *mo ceathrar?*" Fiona asked. Maggie smiled shyly at her cousin, nodding.

✳✳✳✳✳✳✳✳✳✳✳✳✳✳✳✳✳✳✳✳✳✳✳✳✳✳✳✳✳✳

On Friday, Maggie slept until three in the afternoon, and then rushed to ready herself for her date. Surveying her closet, she realized that she was grossly under-wardrobed for a date, and frantically shuffled her clothing around on the rack. She was interrupted by a throat clearing behind her and, startled, spun around to see her cousin watching her.

"Havin' trouble findin' an outfit, dearie?" she asked. Maggie was a little embarrassed, but decided there was no help for it, and nodded at Fiona.

"Okay, who is it tha' ye're goin' out with, and where will ye be goin'?"

Maggie explained the situation, and then awaited her cousin's response.

"I think I ha' jus' the thing fer ya," she said, turning on her heels to leave Maggie's bedroom. Maggie stared at the space her cousin had just occupied, curious to see the garb she would bring back.

Shortly, Fiona emerged from the hallway carrying a beautiful, shimmering piece of fabric. When she held it up for Maggie's inspection, she saw that it was a sexy and gorgeous dress. Maggie held it up against her body and studied her reflection in the mirror.

"Come on, try it on, love," Fiona encouraged, as she began pulling Maggie's shirt up, prompting Maggie to assist her.

The dress donned, Maggie stared at her reflection in awe. It fit her perfectly, as though it was made for her, hugging her curves in all the right places.

"Stunning!" Fiona beamed from behind. Maggie wasn't used to dressing up and loved the way she looked in the dress. She couldn't take her eyes off of herself for a moment, but then remembered that she needed to shower, and knew that it would take a fair amount of time and effort to make her hair presentable.

"Help me get it off," she told her cousin. When Fiona made no move to help, she explained, "I've got to shower and shave."

After blinking, she assisted Maggie in pulling the dress off, asking, "What are ye goin' to do wit' yer hair, love?"

Maggie studied her hair in the mirror and then shrugged, admitting, "I don't fix my hair very often, and it's so long and thick. I don't know of much I can do with it."

Fiona nodded. "I figured as much." When Maggie looked at her, surprised by the comment, Fiona elaborated. "I only meant that ye're hair is so lustrous and healthy, and ye donut get that from over doing it with products all the time, dearie."

Maggie smiled at the explanation, then made her way to the bathroom after wrapping a towel around herself.

After her shower, Maggie went to work on the laborious process of drying her hair. To her delight, it only took forty-five minutes. When she opened the door, Fiona was waiting for her, motioning for her to walk back into the bathroom. "I've got ye're hair taken care of," she explained, pointing to the toilet and prompting Maggie to seat herself.

An hour later, Maggie caught her breath as she took in her reflection. Her cousin had pinned her hair into an up do, adorning it strategically with clips and beautifully decorated pins. "It's beautiful! Thank you!" She closed her mouth, and then opened it, stammering, "I don't think it has ever looked this good before. Ever."

Fiona smiled graciously, pleased with her handy work. "Wha' about ye're make up, me dear?" she asked.

Maggie scutinized herself in the mirror, trying to decide what she would do with her face. Finally, she responded, "I'm not sure. What do you think?"

Fiona smiled at her, and then reached into her bag and pulled out a small lumpy pouch. "I've got it right here, and let's see...ye're about my shade, so that will do just fine." She rummaged through the pouch, removing various items and placing them on the counter.

As she worked on her masterpiece, she wouldn't allow Maggie to look in the mirror until its completion. The two sat silently as Fiona worked, until finally, she added some finishing touches. "There!" she said proudly, stepping back and admiring a job well done.

Turning her to face the mirror gave Maggie a view of herself, and she felt transformed as if by magic. In fact, as she took in the beauty of her hair and makeup, she felt like a Disney princess, and was excited to put the dress back on.

As if reading her mind, her cousin asked, "Shall we dress ye then, *mo ceathrar*?" At this, they went to the bedroom, and Fiona carefully helped Maggie to pull the dress over her head.

Once Maggie was dressed, both women stood back and marveled at her reflection. "Ye're stunning, love," Fiona told her, and then asked, "what shoes do ye have to wear with this get up?"

Maggie hadn't even thought of shoes in the whirlwind of her makeover, and she nearly began to panic. Most of her wardrobe consisted of scrubs and athletic shoes; she simply didn't go out often.

"Not ter worry, dearie. I've got that covered too. What size do ye wear? Looks like about an eight, or nine?"

Shocked that her cousin was such an astute judge of her size, she nodded, continuing to stare at her reflection. When Fiona returned it was with a dazzling pair of high heels that fit the dress perfectly- both in color and in style. Maggie knew she had never been a fashionista, but she certainly could sense the presence of the beauty and style, and was thankful that she and her cousin were so similarly built.

Sitting on the bed, she tried the shoes and was delighted that they were a very close fit. Though they were a bit tight, she realized it was better that they were a touch too small rather than too large. Too big, and she would be fighting to keep them on with every step, and rubbing blisters in her heels.

"Now walk around some," Fiona urged excitedly, adding, "And walk into the living room. Let ye're da see you."

Maggie did as instructed, and her father's gasp told her all she needed to know about her appearance. Not surprisingly, after the way they had bonded, he demanded as he began to move into an upright position, "Now who is the lucky man tha' 'twill be takin' *mo inion* out toni', wit' her lookin' such a bonnie sight?"

Maggie's first instinct was to laugh, certain he was teasing, but then she stopped abruptly, when she realized that he was serious.

"We'el?" he demanded, causing Maggie to blush. For a moment, she almost became defensive at her father's question, but quickly decided that she appreciated his protectiveness. "He's the doctor that cared for my mom. We're going to a medical gala, and he's the guest of honor," she explained.

Maggie wondered if he would want more information about David when he put her curiosity to rest, asking, "When do I get ter meet this guy?"

"You want to meet him, really?" At this, Seamus stood up, and stated, "Yes, I do! If he's tae take *mo*, that is, me daughter out, I would indeed like ta meet 'im."

Maggie could see that he was getting worked up. After some deliberation, she sighed and conceded, "All right. I was going to meet him there, but I suppose I could have him pick me up here instead so that we can see if he meets your qualifications." She said the last word with a giggle, but he didn't seem to notice as he nodded at her and moved in preparation for the introduction.

She sent David a quick text asking him to come get her. His response was immediate: *I can certainly do that. Have yourself ready in 45 minutes.* She replied that she would, and then headed to the kitchen for a drink. She wasn't sure how the evening would go, but knew it would be better with some booze on board.

Maggie fidgeted around, expending some of the nervous energy that had become pent up. She washed the dishes while sipping scotch; wiped down the countertops and took a big swallow; and tossed out some old leftovers before downing the remainder of her drink.

By the time Seamus emerged from the bathroom in a cloud of vapor, she was feeling quite buzzed, and glad for it. Her father's intense gaze, she thought, would quell even the strongest person, and did nothing to calm her frazzled nerves. She felt queasy for a moment, but chased the sensation with another large drink of scotch, checking the time. David was due to arrive in about fifteen minutes.

"He can be quite intimidating in this mode, cousin," Fiona whispered in her ear, as though reading her mind. She then warned, "Ye're friend best be on his bes' behavior, or else he's sure ter get an earful, if not a thrashin'."

Maggie took another large swig and set her glass down just before the doorbell rang.

Seamus made it to the door before either of the ladies had a chance to react. He was wearing nothing but a towel that was wrapped around his waist, but was no less imposing for lack of clothing; in fact he may have been more so. Maggie and Fiona stood watching as he puffed out his muscular chest.

As Maggie observed her father, she appreciated the masculine grace with which he carried himself. Their interactions thus far had been carried out while he was clothed, of course, and during much of that time they had been enveloped in their own grief. Maggie now saw him in a different light, and thought that he was not unlike Shannon in build and in coloring. The thought made her blush and she looked away from her father.

Fiona seemed to read her mind again, remarking, "Ye're da is a good lookin' man, and the ladies do seem to take notice of him. Not that he ever has anything to do wit' them, though it's a pity." Maggie nodded in understanding and went into the living room to listen to her father's discussion with her date, taking a glass of scotch with her.

Seamus sat on her mother's bed and David made himself comfortable on the couch. Her father was still clad in only a towel, and Maggie was sure that if her date was inclined to look, he could easily view her father's genitals. She wondered if he did it on purpose as an intimidation tactic, but seated herself next to him regardless, not wishing to see that part of him.

"David Schambaugh?" Seamus asked, shaking David's hand firmly. David gave a slight nod and a brief smile, answering, "Yes. Or Dr. Schambaugh. Whichever you prefer, and I'll take good care of your daughter, sir. I promise."

Maggie observed the interaction between sips of scotch and decided that David was certainly smooth, and was handling himself quite well through the interrogation. She gave her father a sidelong look, wondering what dads normally asked of men who dated their daughters. The experience was a novel one for her; her mother had always stayed away when men came to pick her up, and she was completely unaccustomed to a parental figure showing interest or concern over her dates.

"I suppose ye take women out quite often, doctor?" he asked, saying the last word as though the feel of it on his tongue disgusted him. David smiled as if he understood where Seamus was coming from. "Not so much as one might think, sir. Working as a neurology Fellow keeps me extremely busy, and there just isn't much time for socializing with the exception of these types of necessary events."

Seamus nodded and looked at David questioningly. In response to his unasked question, David explained, "I'm being presented tonight with an award for humanitarian efforts for my role in treating African victims of violence inflicted by rebels." The room grew quiet at his statement, until he elaborated, "You see, Africa is unfortunately a country where rape is rampant, as is maiming of the victim. I did a stint there for about a month, offering my services for free to the survivors."

The room was again quiet, and Maggie decided that it was likely because no one quite knew how to respond to the sensitive topic David was discussing. Desiring to change the subject, she offered, "Wow, so they're recognizing you with a humanitarian award? That's a great accomplishment, David! Congratulations!"

He turned toward Maggie, startled, as if just then realizing she was in the room. He nodded and exclaimed, "You look gorgeous tonight! Dazzling!" he complimented her as he stood up, took her hand, and kissed it.

In her buzzed mind-state, she let him pull her to her feet as he held onto her hand. Her father stood, kissed her, and gave her a quick embrace. Looking over her shoulder, she saw him fix her date with a glare that said he was not above inflicting bodily harm.

David smiled arrogantly in response, took her from her father, and the two made a hasty exit.

Once in David's car, Maggie couldn't resist admiring herself in the mirror. She had a decent buzz and felt as though she was on top of the world. She was on a date with a handsome doctor who seemed to be at least somewhat into her; she looked fabulous- in fact, better than she could remember ever looking- and when she reflected on everything that had occurred that day, she was pleasantly surprised to realize that Shannon had not crossed her mind once. At least, not until that moment, when she was in awe of her own reflection, wishing he could see her looking so stunning.

"I think I'd like to stop at my house and get a couple of drinks," her date suddenly announced. She nodded while the Porsche made its way toward his apartment in Bricktown.

When they arrived, he poured drinks for both of them, and to her surprise, it was scotch. "How did you know I like scotch?" she asked, smiling curiously.

David smirked at her question, answering sarcastically, "I'm no psychic, Maggie, but even I could smell the scotch on you when I picked you up."

She took a sip while mulling over his response. "Hmmm, that obvious, huh?" He seemed to ignore her remark, but topped off her glass.

After several drinks, they returned to his car. By this time, Maggie was fairly intoxicated. The drive to the gala was a blur, where she was anchored to reality only by David's sporadic comments and the pop music that blared through the sports cars sound system.

At dinner, Maggie slowed her drinking and began to feel tired for it. She assumed David must have perceived this, because he ordered her a coffee drink just in time for her to become slightly more alert during his acceptance speech. She listened as he talked about his work, adding the obligatory humble line here and there, but was still drunk enough that she was having difficulty following him. In fact, she caught herself nodding off once or twice and hoped he didn't notice.

As the evening wore on, she became disappointed when her inebriation began to decrease to the point that she began thinking about Shannon. She wondered what he was doing at that moment, and if he was happy with his wife. As she thought the W word, she could feel bile entering her throat, and took a deep sip to stifle it.

"I said I would like to dance, or are you too drunk to pull that off?" David snapped irritably. Surprised, Maggie turned to look at him, took a sip, and offered an apology. "I'm sorry, David; I was distracted. I'd love to dance with you."

He stood up and stiffly held his hand out to her. She took the proffered limb, and the two walked together toward the dance floor. The song was a slow one and he led, holding her tight against his body. Although she didn't mind his close proximity, she felt that he was being a bit rough with her, though she continued to allow him to lead.

As the dance wore on, David moved them faster, and Maggie became dizzy, until the song finally came to an end. Maggie was relieved, thinking that their dance was over. However, another song quickly followed, and he clutched her even tighter than before, snapping her foggy brain to attention. She pulled away slightly, only to have him pull her harder against him.

"You're hurting me," she exclaimed, attempting to pull away from him.

Maggie thought he would surely let her go, but when she looked up at him, the look in his eyes told a different, more sinister story. It was somehow both angry and vacant at the same time. Maggie suddenly realized that she was afraid of what she saw in him. In her frightened state, she struggled frantically to get away from him, but to no effect.

Not only did her struggles prove fruitless, he pulled her impossibly closer and kissed her on the lips while he groped her bottom, crushing her into his budding erection. She was shocked that not only was he being so rough and inappropriate with her in plain view of everyone in the vast room, but also that he was doing it against her will. When she finally managed to get her wits about her, she bit his tongue with all of her might, drawing blood into her mouth in the process.

By the time David relaxed his hold on Maggie, they were near the door through which they had entered, and he all but dragged her out of the ballroom. She attempted to drag her feet, but was altogether unsuccessful, as his strength was vastly superior to hers.

"Let me go!" she screamed, when she finally found her voice. By that time, they were away from the crowd, and in fact, as she looked around more carefully, she realized that they were alone in a deserted hall.

Maggie fought to get away from David, slapping his back and trying to kick him. But she quickly came to the realization that her resistance was getting her nowhere; in fact, it seemed to encourage him.

When she discovered that he was intent on taking her somewhere, she frantically looked around for a potential rescuer, but saw that they were in a secluded hallway. Eventually, they crossed paths with the valet she recognized from earlier. She cried out to him, only to have David clasp his hand tightly over her mouth, leaving her powerless against his strength, and unable to escape from the powerful grip he had on her.

Over her muffled pleas for assistance, Maggie heard him explain to the valet, "My wife is very drunk. Just ignore her." After a grunt escaped his own throat, likely from Maggie's efforts to bite his hand, he added, "She does this every time, and I always end up having to carry her home."

To her horror, the valet ignored her struggling form and asked, "You ready for your car then, sir?"

"Yes. Please pull my Porsche around," David instructed as he effortlessly held Maggie in a submissive chokehold. The valet disappeared as Maggie writhed, trying to force her teeth into his smothering and encompassing hand.

It suddenly occurred to Maggie that she needed to reach her cell phone. One of her hands left the struggle that was occurring by her throat, and she groped around her hips, searching for her phone, which had been in the pocket of her dress.

"Looking for this, slut?" David hissed, holding her phone in front of her terrified eyes and her quickly-fading vision. She made a desperate grab for it with both hands, but he in turn increased the pressure on her throat.

"I was able to take it from you so easily because of how drunk you were, Maggie," he whispered in her ear, ending the statement with a sound that was somewhere between a sneer and a laugh. He nipped her ear hard enough to draw blood, and continued. "Only whores get that drunk in public, and whores need me to punish them and teach them a lesson. But don't worry, you'll learn your lesson by the time I'm through with you."

She fought to stay alert, but soon the lack of oxygen from asphyxia overcame her, and she lost consciousness.

Maggie eventually awakened to a comfortable somnolence in an unknown bed. As she became more coherent, she had the shocking realization that she was nude, enveloped in the silk sheets in which she lay. Thinking it a dream, and unable to stay awake any longer through the gray that intermittently covered her sight, she settled once more into the oblivious dream state from which she had just emerged.

Sometime later, the fog began to lift, and Maggie realized that something was being forced into her body; she was being violated outside of her control. She suddenly felt extreme pain that was centered in the region of her mid-section. As she slowly began to come around to her conscious self, she realized that the horrible throbbing was occurring in her genitals. "Ung," she cried out without thought. However, the graying of her world mercifully returned, and she was unable to stay awake.

After an unknown amount time had passed, the dimness receded enough that when she turned her face into the pillow, she came to. It suddenly dawned on her that along with the sensations on her face, she was naked. "Wha…" she managed to mutter, before the pain that rocked her became more forceful, cutting off all coherent thought.

Stunned and in disbelief, Maggie realized that there was an invasion of her body occurring. She could feel something thrusting into her, rhythmically. She could feel hot, moist breath bursting onto her breast with each gyration. Gradually, she came to the understand that her body was being used without her consent and despite her lack of consciousness. She felt the excruciating pain shooting through her pubic region. Fighting to push aside the agony, and with a sense of purpose, she somehow managed to will herself back into the relative comfort of the gray nothingness.

She did not awaken for quite some time.

****

Seamus and Fiona sat anxiously in the home of Maggie and her late mother for some time, worrying over Maggie's fate. They each had an ominous feeling about the doctor who had been her date for the evening, although it was easier to complain about it than to try to pinpoint their uneasiness; it was "just a feeling," after all, and neither could say exactly what had caused it.

They spent hours awaiting her return home, spending their energy in a conscious effort to remain calm. By one in the morning, they realized their efforts were in vain, and they both began pacing frantically. They each made guesses about Maggie's fate in an attempt to alleviate their worrisome concerns.

Finally, around two-thirty in the morning, Seamus picked up the phone and began to dial 911. In Ireland, pubs could be open til four, but he was certain that two was the latest in America. Before the first ring was complete, a noise from outside stopped him, and he and Fiona rushed to the front door.

A car peeled out as they opened it. Initially confused by the commotion, they missed the body that was crumpled at their feet. It wasn't until Maggie moaned that they took notice of her.

"My God!" Seamus screamed, before stooping down to gather her up. The elegant dress she had been wearing was wet and ripped in several places. When Seamus got her to her mother's bed, he could see that the dress was soaked in blood. He wrapped the comforter around her to warm her frigid body, and gently rubbed her face to try and rouse her.

Fiona was already on the phone working to get an ambulance en route. When dispatch answered, she responded in a shaky voice, "I need an ambulance here, and police right away."

The question that came next stumped her for a moment, and she yelled to her uncle, "Wha's the address, Uncail?"

Thinking quickly, he went to the drawer of the table in the corner of the living room. After rummaging through it, he located mail addressed to his daughter. Blurting it out, he rushed back to Maggie's side.

"Wha's tha'? ... It's my cousin. She's been hurt badly and... raped." She said the last words very quietly, and then couldn't keep the tears at bay. As little of her cousin as she had seen in the dim light of the living room, somehow she knew with certainty that what she had told the dispatcher was true.

Within a few moments, a flashing red and blue light could be seen through the glass of the screen door, and Fiona rushed to open it. The first police officer she saw was a very tall and broad-shouldered caramel-skinned man. She shrunk back at the sight of him, concerned that her cousin would not want a male to be anywhere near her. But when he spoke, her opinion quickly changed, as she heard the richness of his soft spoken words.

"I'm Officer Johnson. Can you show me where your cousin is?" She nodded, stepping back to allow him inside.

When Johnson took in Maggie's battered form, Fiona saw a chill run through him. He quickly backed up and yelled through the door for the ambulance to hurry.

The time it took to get her onto the gurney passed in a blur as Fiona and Seamus moved around the crowded room in an attempt to stay out of the way. Once she was loaded into the ambulance, Fiona went to accompany her, only to be told by the medic that she could not. In answer, Fiona held her head high and stated in a commanding tone, "I let her out of my sight with a man I didna ken, and this is wha' happent to her. I'll no be makin' tha same mistake again."

When he argued with her, the other medic, presumably with more experience, came around and told his co-worker, "Let her pass. We're wasting time here. I want to get this one delivered quickly."

"Fine," the first one spurted, "but you best stay out of my way," mustering as much authority as his skinny little frame would allow.

Fiona wasn't at all upset about being talked to like a child. She pulled herself into the cave of the ambulance and settled herself in at Maggie's head, stroking her face and struggling to choke back the tears. It was the first good view she had of the swelling and bruising, and it was no small feat to keep her emotions from engulfing her.

She was glad she was there, nonetheless, and was adamant that she would not leave her cousin's side if it was at all possible. While she gave what small comforts she could to Maggie's unconscious form, the medic worked to start an IV, placing a warming blanket over her.

In no time, they arrived at the hospital and Maggie was taken into a large bay where a multitude of medical staff began working on her. Fortunately, Fiona felt that she was in good hands, but unfortunately, she had to leave, and was taken to a small family room where she awaited news of her cousin's fate in solitude.

****

At Maggie's home, the officer discussed what little information Seamus had about the person she had been with. Seamus remembered his name perfectly, and recited it for the officer, and then described in great detail the way he looked, walked, and talked. He then told him what Maggie had said about him being the doctor who had cared for her mother. Rummaging through the drawer again helped him to locate an envelope addressed to Maggie's mother that appeared to be a medical bill.

"Maybe this 'ill help, Officer. It's from OU Medical Center. If it's where she was treated, then it mus' be where this wee bastard works."

Johnson took the envelope from him and opened it, examining the bill inside. "Dr. David Schambaugh, you say?" the officer asked.

"Aye," Seamus nodded, which prompted the officer to turn the bill around for his inspection. On the top corner of the bill, the name of the doctor who had taken his daughter out was printed in black and white. "Got 'im." Seamus exclaimed.

The two moved toward the door at this point. Johnson opened the front passenger door, shepherding Seamus into his cruiser, and then got in himself. Immediately, he went to work perusing records in his vehicle's computer.

Seamus watched as the officer searched, noting the information on the monitor. When he saw the listed address for the doctor, he focused intently on it for several moments, burning it into his memory.

"You have a good eye for detail, Mister?" the officer asked, and Seamus realized that he knew he had seen the bastard's address.

"Ye can call me Seamus."

"Do you think you would recognize this guy if I showed him to you?"

He watched him for a moment, as though sizing him up. Seamus wasn't sure, but he thought the officer didn't seem to be the type to mind what he would do if he got his hands on the guy who had brutalized his daughter. "Aye," he answered, "tha' I can."

Confirmation received, Johnson backed his car out of the driveway, and the two made their way toward Bricktown. Seamus wondered what was happening with his daughter. She had looked to be in rather poor shape, and he was terrified for her.

As he rode in silence with the officer, he nervously drummed his fingers on his thigh. The adrenaline was coursing through his veins, his heart pounding in his chest. Despite the presence of the officer, he wasn't sure he could keep his hands from the man who had hurt his little girl, though he wasn't entirely certain that he wanted to stop himself.

Finally, they arrived at a sophisticated looking apartment building. Johnson checked in with dispatch, and then told Seamus to remain in the car. It took all of his self-control to comply with the demand, but he was reasonably certain that Johnson would not apprehend Doctor Dick while alone with him there. *Smart man,* he thought, with grudging approval.

Several moments later, Johnson returned empty-handed. "No one home," he told Seamus. "But Dr. Schambaugh's car is here, and it's been left unlocked. Do you happen to know where it was that they went on their date?"

Seamus, glad to at least have knowledge of where the man lived, was ready to see how his daughter was doing, and shook his head that he did not. It had the desired effect, and Officer Johnson said, "Very well, I'll take you to the hospital."

As they rode together, Johnson explained the process that would likely take place within the course of the investigation. "They took your daughter to the right place, if what I suspect happened to her actually did. Baptist Medical Center is where they're conducting SANE exams this month."

Seamus let out a small grunt at the word "sane," prompting the officer to explain. "Not "sane" as in 'insane'. SANE, s-a-n-e. It stands for sexual assault nurse exam, and it's a forensic exam where a specially-trained nurse will collect evidence from your daughter." When Seamus still appeared unsure, he promised, "Your daughter is in good hands, sir. These ladies know what they're doing and they treat the victim right. And it's the best way to get this guy if that's what happened to her."

He blinked at the information before asking, "Then wha' will be happenin' to me daughter? And wha' will be happenin' to this doctor guy?"

Johnson took a deep breath before emphatically explaining, "This shit bag will be put away for a long time if I have anything to do with it." His rich baritone and his statement helped to reassure Seamus, but what he said next gave room to doubt.

"It's not all up to me, but I'll personally do everything I can to see him held responsible. Next the case will be presented to the detectives. In Oklahoma City, there are specific detectives who are assigned to major crimes such as rape and murder. Your daughter's case will fall into one of the major crime categories, most likely, so they will be contacting you within the next couple of days. After that…" he paused briefly to observe an erratic driver, but then continued. "After that, the district attorney's office will decide whether or not to prosecute the guy, depending on the evidence that's found. The DA's office has special people as well that specifically handle major violent cases. Its better this way because they have a better understanding of the dynamics involved in these types of crimes."

Seamus struggled to process the information as a sense of foreboding set in. If his calculations were correct, his daughter's case would have to go through a small army before it stood a chance of the guy being prosecuted, and would include her having to testify, if he correctly understood America's criminal justice system. The adrenaline rushed through him as he continued drumming his fingers on his thigh. He kept repeating Doctor Dick's address in his head as he stared forward without seeing anything in front of him.

Chapter Fourteen

Jasmine awakened to the repeated ringing of the doorbell. Staring blearily at her alarm clock, she squinted to bring the electronic numbers into focus. Aroused so abruptly from the deep sleep she had finally achieved, she was alarmed; persistently ringing door bells at four a.m. were most certainly not the bearer of good news.

Jumping out of bed, she ran downstairs, taking the steps two at a time. Patrick wasn't with her on this night. Instead, he was sleeping at the hospital as they tried to determine whether the issues that had plagued him recently, as well as earlier in his life, were the result of a medical condition.

As she flung open the front door, Jasmine was again surprised: both of her children were there, being held by her husband. One look at his pale, stricken face told her that the circumstances were disastrous.

"Morgan's friend has been badly hurt, Jasmine. Can ye take the children for the night?"

Jasmine backed away from him while reaching for her younger daughter in an effort to lighten his load. "Of course, John. Lay Deirdre down there," she answered in a sympathetic tone, gesturing to the couch that still sat in the room's entryway.

Her younger daughter snuggled against her breast while John settled Deirdre against the plush cushions. Tucking her neatly under the blanket he had pulled from the back of the sofa, he stood, turning to go. "Thank you, Jasmine; I'll call you later…" he trailed off, sprinting toward his awaiting car.

She went back to the door, watching the vehicle pull out of her driveway. The dim light of the interior gave little away, though she thought she could see Morgan's face, which was clearly distraught.

Retreating to the sofa, Jasmine lay her sleeping child on the end opposite her sister, sitting silently to muse over the recent turn of events. She would be picking up her beloved in several hours. She wondered how he was faring with his sleep study, deciding that that space of time could be momentous, not only for her, but for her husband as well.

As she moved away from her younger child, her arm was gripped, alerting her to the fact that Callie was not, in fact, asleep. "Mommy cuddle with me?" Callie asked drowsily.

Jasmine took her place next to the babe, grateful for the respite she had always felt while snuggling with her children. "Yes, my little cutie patootie. Mommy will cuddle with you." She spoke the words softly to the top of her child's head, resting her chin on top of her as she settled into the couch, resigned to a sleepless morning.

Had she been awake enough to notice, she would've been surprised when sleep actually came.

****

Arriving in the emergency room, Morgan's heart was in her throat. She had barely muttered three words since receiving the call from her best friend's newly-found cousin.

This isn't real. Maggie doesn't even have a cousin named Fiona, she kept telling herself, praying it was all a huge misunderstanding. If she kept thinking this, then when she made it to this so-called Maggie's room, it would be a different Maggie clinging to life; an imposter. And if that was the case, she could call the true Maggie and tell her all about it, and then they would laugh and talk about how frightening it had been. The knot that constricted her throat would go away, and the tears that continued to flow would cease falling uncontrollably.

These thoughts persisted in an endless cycle where she worked fervently to talk herself out of believing in her own reality...until she found herself standing next to Maggie's bed, gazing numbly at her pale, lifeless form.

Upon entering the room, she couldn't stop herself from throwing herself on her friend any more than she could stop the intrusive thoughts that she now knew to be nothing more than desperate wishful thinking. The fact that the unconscious figure didn't hug her back was further proof of the new reality in which Morgan found herself; one where she couldn't discuss things with her most treasured friend. In this moment, life ceased to exist. The earth stopped turning. Morgan's heart stopped beating...

...until she felt gentle hands lifting her up. For a split second, she speculated that she had died and was moving upward towards heaven. She wondered if she would soon reunite with Maggie.

But then, she felt something brush against her face. As if across a great distance, she realized that her lover held her close and it was his chest that her head was leaning against. In her peripheral vision, she could eventually see her legs and her arms. Cocooned under a blanket against John's chest, she was being rocked gently back and forth. In this space of time for her, the world outside of her warm haven did not exist.

Jarring her back into harsh reality was the voice of a man speaking over Maggie's body. "Through this holy anointing, may the Lord in his love and his holy mercy lift you up," the priest was saying, when Morgan threw the blanket away from herself.

"Jocelyn Magnolia Sumner, as you pass from this realm and into the next, may the Lord, with his love and mercy, help you and heal you with the grace of the Holy Spirit." As he said these words over her, he dabbed olive oil on her forehead. Morgan could only watch in mute terror as he read the last rites. Before she could open her mouth to correct him, firm hands gripped her, pulling her back.

Dumbly, Morgan watched as a team of people rushed into the room. As if by force of their collective sheer will, all of the occupants of the room moved away from the gurney on which Maggie lay. The priest, who only moments before was praying over Maggie, seemed to shrink into the wall, only to come alive when a bundle of surgical blue coverings were thrust into his hands.

"You come with us, but put these on first!" he was instructed abruptly, as Maggie's bed was wheeled out. Snapping out of her trance, Morgan watched him don the gear as he simultaneously ran to catch up with the gurney.

Morgan felt that her chest was as empty as the room had become without the bed and its occupant. Her legs crumbling beneath her, she was again thankful for John's strength and presence, as he pulled her onto his lap.

"She's our girl, and she's a strong one. If anyone can make it through this, it's her," Morgan heard a voice whisper, mirroring her own thoughts.

Slowly glancing around the room, she realized that she and her lover were not actually alone. Seated on the floor against the opposite wall was the man from the funeral- Maggie's father, with a red-haired woman sitting next to him. Morgan concluded that she must be Fiona. Part of her wanted to hug the forlorn-looking woman while the other part wanted to kick her. She wasn't sure if it was out of the anger she felt that Fiona had been the one to inform her of her friend's predicament, or jealousy that she had been the one who was there to assist her in her dire time of need.

Her thoughts were abruptly halted when the woman stood, crossing the room to her.

"I'm Fiona, dearie…Maggie's cousin. I talked to ye on the phone," she explained. As much as Morgan wanted to decline the warmth being offered, she stepped into Fiona's embrace. Losing control of her tightly wound emotions, she burst into tears, returning the hug. The two held on, crying into the other's shoulder.

Finally, they each breathed and released each other, and Morgan stepped back into the security of John's arms.

"I thought they were nice last rites he read," Fiona breathed aloud, as Morgan was held by her lover.

The observation had Morgan feeling as though she needed to correct the mistake she had heard earlier. "It was nice, yes, but he had her name wrong. Maggie always hated the name 'Magnolia.' She would've had it changed a long time ago had it not been for her mom."

As soon as the words had left her mouth, Maggie's father perked up a bit. Smiling wryly, he asked, "Her mum named her that, did she?"

Morgan turned to him, confused by his suddenly cheery tone.

He must have noticed, as he explained, "We fell in love at Magnolia Cottage, we did, and it was there tha' Maggie was conceived." His eyes had taken on a faraway dreamy look as he recalled, and Morgan wondered if he was reliving the moment in his head.

His musing was interrupted when Fiona elbowed him in the side, saying good-naturedly, "Ye've embarrassed yerself again, Seamus…these nice people donut want to hear about ye're long lost love."

He reached over, ruffling her hair before kissing her on the cheek. "This one doesna let me get away wit' much these days," he stated, smiling fondly at his niece.

As the gay moment died down, the group waited quietly in the ER bay for news of Maggie's condition. Unfortunately, it would be a long wait for them.

****

When Jasmine arrived at the hospital to collect her beloved, it was with a storm of emotions brewing under the surface. On one hand, being separated from Patrick for so long had been difficult, and she missed him terribly. Admittedly, they had only been apart for eight hours, but since she had finally gotten him to herself after so many years of yearning, any time away was too much. On the other hand, she worried that the outcome of the sleep study in which he had participated could be damaging to their relationship.

Arriving at the external door of the facility, Jasmine was surprised to see a bandaged Patrick with a series of bruises and cuts on his face and hands. When she became upset, he waved away her concern, taking his place in the passenger seat, explaining, "Ye were right, dearie, I ha' been brawlin' because of me lack of sleep."

Jasmine studied him, confused by the contradictions she saw. The smile on his face and sparkle in his eyes was in stark contrast to his bruised and bloodied face and hands. When he reached over, placing his arm around her and pulling her in for a hearty hug, it suddenly dawned on her that the things which she had worried about were no longer a concern.

"It's true then, my love?" Jasmine asked hopefully, returning the hug. Patrick responded by kissing her; a slowly simmering passionate display, which had him pulling her from her seat, and into his lap.

"I love ye so much, me love. Ye ha' given me something so monumental…a gift beyond words, and I canna ever repay ye, me love," he whispered, caressing her cheek just before taking possession of her lips again.

They held each other tightly, caressing exposed skin while exploring each other's mouths. His hand soon found its way under her shirt. Fondling her breasts, he settled on her nipples, where he caressed little circles, causing her breath to quicken. She soon began rocking back and forth in his lap, appreciating the blossoming erection she felt against her bottom.

Suddenly, the couple was startled by a loud knock on the car's passenger window. Jasmine glanced down and shockingly realized that her blouse had become unbuttoned, her breasts slightly exposed. As if she'd been bitten in the bottom, she jumped up, quickly returning to the driver's seat.

The expression on the security guard's face as she drove away told her he was not completely dissatisfied with the show he had watched. The idea that there had been an audience, one that had clearly enjoyed watching what she and her lover had been doing, was surprisingly arousing to her, and the ever-present blush on her face crept down to her neck, settling on her already-sensitive breasts.

Patrick must have been feeling the same as he excitedly announced, "That was hot, ya wee vixen! I think the guard got his jollies watchin' ye. An' I canna say I blame him. Look how sexy ye are, my future bride!" He lovingly stroked her heated core, to where his fingers had ventured.

His touch was driving Jasmine's passion up, and she sped toward their destination, nearly unable to contain herself. When he withdrew his fingers, suckling them in his mouth and tasting her, she veered into the oncoming lane from being so turned on. *It's a good thing it's Saturday and there's not much traffic*, she thought.

"You're gonna get us into a collision, Patchy! I cannot take any more of this and still drive us."

Unrepentant, Patrick captured her hand, placing it on his erection. "Then we will be even, my bride. This is what ye are doin' to me body. I want ye so bad it hurts." Where she felt of him, his hardness and size stretched the material of his trousers. Jasmine was immensely pleased and further aroused by this, as his stimulation was a result of the things he had been doing to her, and the pleasure she made him feel.

Regretfully pulling her hand away, Jasmine resolutely placed it on the steering wheel, pointedly keeping her eyes forward. "It will have to wait, my love...just as this will have to wait for you." She said the last bit as she reached down and fondled her clitoris, becoming wetter while her pelvis gyrated against her own finger tips.

Unfortunately, they were still several miles from home. Jasmine increased the vehicle's speed to nearly ninety miles per hour, hoping not to encounter law enforcement.

When they finally made it home, the car was still in drive when Patrick began fondling Jasmine again. She became lost in his touch so quickly that she was interrupted only by the slight jolt when the vehicle bumped into the garage wall. Reacting swiftly, she managed to put the car in park.

While unbuttoning his trousers, Patrick pulled Jasmine from the driver's side and onto his lap, moving the material aside just enough so that he could impale her with his shaft. The two thrust into each other, impassioned, in a frenzy to be joined.

Needing more room to maneuver, the two simultaneously moved toward the driver's seat so that Jasmine was on her hands and knees, Patrick perched over the top of her. The car's center console was the perfect height and place for Jasmine to rest as he pounded into her. She raised her bottom to meet his delicious assault as the two made feverish, passionate love.

With the pressure building, Jasmine gloriously orgasmed, crying out her lover's name. She enticed him so intensely that his release spewed into her seconds later, and they lay resting across the front seat for a moment. Finally she stirred, prompting Patrick to move off of her.

"Holy hell! That was bloody fantastic!" Patrick exclaimed. His passion then simmered, and he leaned in and kissed her slowly, caressing her cheek, as the two savored the feeling and presence of the other.

When their emotions were finally spent, they exited the car together, breathless still from their recent tryst. Arriving in the house to the children, Jasmine felt that her life was complete.

Her sentiment was mirrored in her lover when he pulled her to him, whispering in her ear, "This is it, my love. We begin our life anew. There's nothin' between us and our happiness now."

She held him to her, savoring the feel of him next to her. When they were joined by his mother, he turned Jasmine around, taking a knee in front of her. Stunned by his actions, Jasmine stared down at him, trying to comprehend what he was doing.

"My beloved Jasmine," he said, lovingly grasping her hand in his. Gazing into her eyes, he asked, "Will ye give me the honor of being my bride, me love? I canna live without ye."

Jasmine was speechless, her heart full to bursting at Patrick's proposal. Unable to find her voice, she smiled and nodded excitedly, her eyes filling with tears. He leapt up and placed his lips on hers, passionately embracing and kissing her, before placing a large, elegant ring on her second finger. She stared at it, admiring its beauty and effervescence.

For what seemed like an eternity they were in their own world until the quiet was broken by Callie and Brunne clapping. Her older daughter had a different reaction, however. "My dada won't like this, mommy! You stop kissing her Uncle Patch! Stop kissing her this instant!" Deirdre angrily demanded with a stomp of her little foot, to Jasmine's simultaneous shock and amusement.

"We willna have any of that ye wee goblin. Ye let ye're ma an' uncail enjoy themselves, little one. Ye're da has got his own lil' bit o' happiness fer himself, so donut you be botherin' ye're mum about 'ers." Brunne chided.

To Jasmine's surprise, her mother-in-law had corrected the child on her behalf. She couldn't stop herself from planting a grateful kiss on the old woman's cheek and giving her a hearty hug. Her actions were followed closely by Patrick, and they reveled in a group hug.

The two lovers smiled and began laughing, which provoked chuckles from both Brunne and Callie. Their merriment was contagious and before long, Deirdre joined in.

The rest of the afternoon was filled with joy and laughter; a time that would not soon be forgotten by any of the inhabitants therein.

****

In Maggie's room in the ICU, Morgan made several circuits as she nervously paced the floor. The surgery had gone on for nine long hours; a gut-wrenching period of waiting which seemed as if it would never end. Morgan couldn't stop herself from looking at her friend every other minute, an action that both reassured and frightened her. Maggie's presence, despite the breathing machines and the IV lines that snaked in and out of her body, was a reminder that she was fighting and for the moment remained alive. But the amount of visible damage was evidence of the extent to which the woman had been viciously attacked. The sight of it brought Morgan to the verge of tears each time her eyes rested on her.

Occasionally Maggie would moan, and Morgan rushed to her side with newfound hope mingled with fear. The prognosis was grim, with Maggie having lost three times her total volume in blood throughout the ordeal and subsequent surgery.

While she was grateful that Maggie's life had thus far been spared, Morgan's frustrations continued to mount. Not a single one of the plethora of medical staff could give her concrete information; only "we'll have to wait and see." She just couldn't understand how Maggie's life, which was so vital and important, could be teetering so precariously on the precipice of life and death, with so few answers.

Her interminable cycle of thoughts and pacing ceased when John entered, automatically walking over and embracing her.

As was the case each time he had returned after a short absence, Morgan held him closely, sobbing into his chest.

After they were seated next to each other, John whispered quiet words to her in his native tongue, soothing and caressing her. In her emotional torrent she couldn't quite discern that he was speaking a different language, but the words calmed her nonetheless.

Finally, with no more tears left, Morgan collapsed in emotional exhaustion against her lover, inhaling his breath and his essence, and gaining respite. The energy she had expended in her hysteria coalesced into a peaceful calm that left the room eerily silent; a silence broken only by the occasional beeping of the life-sustaining machines and monitors.

Eventually, John caressed Morgan's face, pushing her hair aside and kissing her forehead. "I have business I must attend to, my love. I would not think to leave you at a time like this, but it is unavoidable," he told her, watching her closely, gauging her reaction to his proposed absence.

She blinked, nodding slightly. Though Morgan hated the idea of his leaving, she knew that his presence would in no way change the outcome of her friend's fate. Besides, in all honesty, she felt that, for some reason, Maggie seemed to hold more steadfastly to life when she was alone with her.

After gaining her acquiescence, John stood and assisted Morgan into the chair, gently wrapping a blanket around her. "I'll be gone only for a short while, *mo shearc*."

Morgan stared at him, comprehension dawning that he meant to leave the hospital altogether. There was a brief twinge of panic as she felt abandoned by her lover: the one person from whom she had been gaining the most comfort in her time of need.

Admittedly, however, he couldn't stay with her forever, and Maggie would likely have a long road ahead.

Standing, she kissed him deeply, passionately, in an attempt to preemptively take as much of him as possible before he left her side. She was unsure how long he would be gone and was afraid to ask; afraid the answer would make his absence unbearable. If she could pretend he would be gone for a short while- perhaps only down the hall- it would be bearable.

He returned her passion and the two embraced for several moments, until he took his leave of her. Watching him go, Morgan sunk back into the chair, tucking herself back under the blanket, and staring at Maggie's sleeping form. Her bedside vigil would continue for quite some time.

Chapter Fifteen

When Maggie finally awakened, she was in a fog from which she struggled to emerge, and in an unfamiliar bed. She attempted to speak but was unsuccessful, as there was something blocking her throat. The resulting movement caused her to erupt into spasms of choking and spurting.

"She's awakin' up!" Maggie heard a voice say close to her ear. Somewhere in the recesses of her brain, she recognized the voice, but couldn't quite place it. Each time she worked to swallow, she choked on the tube. Finally, she was able to free her hand, and reached up and yanked out the plastic that was occluding her airway.

Unfortunately, this merely resulted in a different type of smothering, and she tried desperately to suck in enough oxygen. Luckily, a mask was quickly placed over her face, helping her to calm down, and her breathing gradually returned to normal.

"That's it, deep breaths," a confident, feminine voice assured her. Eventually, she had calmed enough to observe some of the people in the room, and she began to realize that she was surrounded by the familiar faces of people that she loved.

When she moved her head slightly so that she was able to take in more of the room, her heart sped up as she saw none other than Shannon watching her from the corner. She couldn't take her eyes off of him, and it seemed that he was having the same difficulty removing his from her.

Their gaze was interrupted by Morgan stepping into her line of sight. "Oh my gosh, I'm so glad you're awake, Maggie!" she cried ecstatically, not bothering to hold her tears in check.

Maggie smiled up at her friend, and then delved into her memory to try and remember what happened to her, and why she had been intubated. Finally, the oxygen mask was removed from her face, and she was able to look around the room more easily.

The sun gaily rained beams into the room, telling Maggie it must be late morning, or perhaps early afternoon. Looking around the room, she saw that there was a large collection of flowers, balloons, and stuffed animals just outside her door. The stiffness she felt in her limbs suggested that she had lain in bed for quite a long time.

As Maggie saw the anxiety in the faces of the people crowded around her, she began to worry over herself and at last managed to verbalize some of her confusion, although her voice weakly emerged as a thready croak. "What happened...? How did I..?"

Morgan's face turned white at the questions, and Maggie thought she wouldn't answer her. But Morgan turned to the others present in the room and requested, "Why don't you all run to the cafeteria so I can talk to Maggie alone for a bit." Everyone complied, with the exception of Shannon, who stood stubbornly in the corner.

Morgan was about to complain at him, but he cut her off, stating, "I'll no have ye shoving me out like ever one else. I wish ta stay wit' her, and I willna be goin' unless it is wha' she wishes."

Morgan turned to her, and Maggie looked over at Shannon for a moment. She nodded her consent to Morgan, allowing him to remain in the room with them. He moved to sit on the bed next to her, and she found that his presence made her feel secure, steadying her somewhat.

Morgan sat on the other side of the bed and took her hand. "What I am about to tell you will likely be a huge surprise to you, as well as a bit of a shock," Morgan began. She waited for Maggie's reaction, trying to determine her grasp of the situation, but was interrupted when Maggie impatiently demanded, "Just tell me, Morgan. Sitting here with you looking at me like that is scaring me even more."

The last sentence came out as little more than a whisper from Maggie's awareness that whatever it was might, in fact, be that bad, but Morgan hurried all the same to relay to her what had taken place.

"Your date…that bastard doctor…they think he raped you and then hurt you terribly, Maggie."

Shocked, Maggie again searched her brain in an effort to remember something, *anything*. Occasionally, she caught fleeting glimpses of being unable to breathe where she thought she was in water, but none of her memories would stay put, as if she was remembering the foggy details of a dream. It was like trying to catch a fish with tongs, and was nearly as effective.

Shannon gently took Maggie's hand in his and without averting his gaze, told Morgan, "Don't keep the other part from her. She deserves ta know." Maggie watched him watching her, and was swiftly becoming impatient to have the rest of the information shared with her.

Finally, Morgan replied, "I think you should be the one to tell her. It has more to do with you, after all."

Shannon brought his face much closer to Maggie's, and then very quietly told her, "Ye're goin' ta be a mum, Maggie." She was too flabbergasted to speak, and he continued, "When they verra first brought ye here las' week, they did one of those tests, and it was positive at the outset. Then they did the blood test, and it turns out ye're verra early along. I thinks it's me wee babby, love, considerin' all tha' we ha' been doin' before me wife showt up and ruint ever thing."

Maggie's heart pounded at the revelation. She slowly pulled her hand from Morgan's, then automatically placed it over her abdomen in an instinctively protective gesture. As she tried to process all of the new information, she felt dizzy. She had a million questions, but none of them formed coherently in her mind.

Seeing her struggle, Shannon asked her, "Could the babe belong to anyone else, love?"

Maggie nodded her head and answered, "David. It could be his. We…" Before she could confess, the tears began sliding down her cheeks. How could he have done this to her, when she was pregnant? Of course he hadn't known, but she remembered articles she had read previously which had suggested that rape can sometimes a physiological thing done when one male senses somehow that his female is pregnant by a different man. As farfetched as she had always found that theory, her situation made it seem plausible.

Shannon squeezed her hand, and then assured her, "I willna allow ye to raise the babe on ye're own, lass, and I donut care whose it is." His speech slowed down for a moment, and Maggie didn't understand why, until he quietly added, "Tha's unless ye want me to have naught to do wit' it."

Maggie thought her heart would break at his suggestion, remembering his anger over his wife's numerous abortions, and she couldn't keep her hand from reaching up and reassuringly smoothing back his hair. "It would be my honor to have you as the father of my child. But Shannon, is that why, that is…" She stammered, trying to come up with the courage to ask the question, but decided that he probably knew some pretty intimate details about her, considering all that had been revealed. Finally, she finished: "Is that why you've come back? Because I'm pregnant?"

Shannon did not hesitate for one second. Instead, he immediately shook his head, explaining softly, "I never left ye, Maggie. I've been right here all along. I jus' didna let ye know I was near."

When he could see her struggling with another question, he clarified further. "I thought it 'twas quite strange that me wife showt up pregnant after being gone from me fer a bit, an' it turnt out she wasna pregnant after all. So I didna leave wit' her."

Shannon squeezed Maggie's hand as a smile began to appear on his lips, but he then continued more seriously. "I watched ye with ye're da for a while. When he was at ye're house I thought fer sure ye had found someone to replace me already. Then I saw the doctor at ye're door the night of the date, and tried ter put the pieces together. It wasna til after he dropped ye on ye're doorstep tha' way, that I became worrit about him."

With this, he spoke no more, and Maggie suspected that he was keeping something from her. However, she was distracted when Morgan told her, "They're looking for him, Maggie, and I think that as badly as they want to catch this ass hat, they'll find him."

The conversation ended when Seamus entered the room with a woman Maggie did not recognize. She looked disheveled, and as though she hadn't slept in years. The three on the bed looked at him questioningly. He closed the door before she began talking.

"Are you the handiwork of Dr. David Schambaugh, as well?" she asked. When she spoke his name, her face twisted into a bitter sneer, and she commanded the room's attention. Before anyone could respond, she said, "My name's Sam, and I believe my friend was hurt by him as well. She's in the room next door. She's been here a while longer than you."

Sam paused, watching their reactions. The silence was broken when Shannon asked her, "Why do ye think he did somethin' to ye're friend? From what I've overheard o' her, she couldna remember anything tha' happened to her."

Sam gave Shannon a long look, likely appraising him, and trying to decide how much to share. Finally, she confided, "It's my fault, really, that it happened to her." Her eyes began filling with tears, and she had to compose herself before she could continue.

Eventually, she admitted to the group how she had been jealous of Schambaugh and Jordan having sex at work. She had called and threatened him, impersonating Jordan, then she had anonymously reported him for sexually harassing her friend.

When she finished recounting her story, she appeared more tired than before, yet seemed relieved all the same.

"So you see, if I hadn't baited him, he probably wouldn't have done that to her."

Morgan looked thoughtful for a moment before responding. "Even though what you did was wrong, *he* is the only one responsible for what happened, not you. Thank you for sharing, though." She turned away from Sam and back toward Maggie, dismissing her.

"Thank you for that. I feel really shitty about what I did." She looked around the room for a moment, and then asked, "So what are they doing to catch this son of a bitch?"

This time, Seamus answered her, fiercely stating, "They donut know where the bloody bastard is, but don't ye worry. If I get me hands on 'im first, they willna need to worry about 'im any longer."

As soon as the words had left his mouth, a silent exchange took place between Shannon and Seamus. Sam left the room, closing the door behind her.

Morgan exhaled a frustrated sigh. "I *cannot* believe some of the outrageous things people do!"

"Mmmph," Shannon grunted in agreement before returning his attention to Maggie. "I donut suppose ye'd have any objections to me hurtin' the da of ye're child, if it isna me?"

Maggie was again surprised at the reminder of the idea of parenthood, but nevertheless shook her head in consent.

With that, Shannon stood up and motioned for Seamus to follow him outside, leaving the two women to themselves.

"So, how bad was it?" Maggie asked quietly. As she awaited Morgan's response, she focused on her hands as they twisted in and out of the sheet that covered her.

Morgan again looked thoughtful as if considering how to answer the question before she could speak. She then stated, giving very little inflection, "Very bad, Maggie. We almost lost you twice."

Maggie absorbed the information, feeling lightheaded once again. "No, I mean, how bad did he…rape me, Morgan? What did he do?"

Morgan drew a quick breath, giving her much of the answer she needed, but Maggie waited patiently for the whole story.

After a pause, Morgan began talking. "You had to be taken to surgery, and they were unsure if you could hold onto the pregnancy. You had to be transfused with several units of blood." She took a deep breath before continuing. "They think he used some type of instrument on you. The damage just couldn't be explained by a penis. And your...butt...that's where the majority of the damage was. Otherwise, the baby probably wouldn't have survived."

Maggie began wriggling around as she worked to sit up for the first time since she had awakened. Prodding herself in random places, she worked to gauge any pain or tenderness. When she reached her genital area, then lifted up to feel her bottom, she gingerly touched herself. Surprisingly, there wasn't any pain; only the slightest tenderness.

"How long have I been out?" she asked, thinking of the question for the first time.

Morgan looked at her sadly, admitting, "About four days. If you're not feeling pain down there any more, that might be why." Morgan's expression told Maggie that she expected her to become upset, but instead she seemed relieved.

When Morgan looked at her curiously, Maggie explained, "I'm glad I didn't have to feel any pain or remember what happened, Morgan. I know it sounds strange that not knowing would be better, but to know it, and have to remember something that horrible happening...I just think it would have made it more difficult to deal with."

Morgan nodded, and after a brief pause acknowledged, "I think you're right about that being the best thing for you, but for some people, maybe it's better to know."

Before anything else could be said on the subject, the door opened, and a cheerful nurse entered, with Seamus, Shannon, John, and Fiona behind her. "You're awake!" the nurse exclaimed to her patient. "How are you feeling? Any pain?"

Maggie shook her head. "No, none at all, actually."

"Well, that's good. The detectives are wanting you to call them as soon as you wake up. That is…if you feel up to talking to them just yet." The nurse's energy invigorated Maggie somewhat, and she felt that she might in fact be up to speaking with them.

As Shannon squeezed in next to her on the bed, settling his arm around her waist, her father stood on the other side holding her hand, and Fiona seated herself at the foot, facing her. John put his arm around Morgan as the two positioned themselves behind Fiona, and the group quietly enjoyed each other's presence. Maggie was self-conscious, but positioned herself against Shannon, her face against his chest and her eyes closed. As she breathed him in, she felt whole, and could not remember a time she had ever felt more at peace.

****

Maggie was lucky that she was set to be discharged within the next couple of days. However, Jordan was not as fortunate. Although she eventually emerged from her coma, she was never the same, and had to spend much of her remaining adult life living with family. She went on to develop agoraphobia, unable to leave her house without suffering severe panic and anxiety attacks.

Chapter Sixteen

On Wednesday, Maggie was discharged by early morning. She had grown restless of late, cooped up in the small hospital room. Even surrounded by her family and loved ones as she was, she craved a change of scenery and some fresh air.

As she ducked into the passenger seat of her car, Shannon turned to her from behind the steering wheel, stating, "Ye're finally free, love. Where would ye like to go?"

She thought for a moment, realizing that she really did feel like she had been freed from some terrible prison. She looked him in the eye, emphatically declaring, "I would love nothing more than to go with you to John's house."

He leaned over and kissed her, expressing his joy of being with her, and set off toward his old friend's house.

When they arrived, Shannon swept her into his arms, carrying her over the threshold, and whispering in her ear, "It feels like home, love."

She looked up at him, wide-eyed, and unsure of what he meant by the remark. He responded to her unasked question, "It's where I first met you, and 'tis where I made love to ye so thoroughly. Tis home for me."

She pushed lightly on his chest so that he would set her down, and then stood on her tiptoes to reach his mouth with hers. Wrapping her arm around his neck, she pulled him in for a kiss, and the rest of the world ceased to exist.

They practically made love with their mouths, until a loud clearing of a throat prompted them to notice that they were not alone. Reluctantly, they released each other, turning around to survey their surroundings.

Morgan and John were standing next to the stairs watching them. Maggie smiled and blushed brightly, but Shannon's countenance was smug as he possessively held her in his arms.

"Did you forget that we have work to do, my friend?" John asked, feigning impatience.

Unabashedly, he leaned down and kissed Maggie deeply again. He then walked her to her friend. "He's right love. There's business tha's needin' taken care of." He kissed her one last time, and then regrettably left her by the foot of the stairs, where she was watching him walk with John toward his study.

"How are you feeling?" Morgan asked Maggie, pulling her in for a hug. After the embrace, she stepped back and looked again at her friend. "Look at you! You're glowing! Pregnancy definitely suits you, Maggie. And it's about time! I knew my kids would wind up babysitting your kids, but I didn't think I'd be close to having grandkids before it happened!"

"Shut up!" Maggie laughed, playfully smacking her friend's arm. "I really do feel good, and Shannon makes me feel so... cherished."

Morgan's smile was nearly as bright as Maggie's. "I know exactly what you mean. John makes me feel the same way. And he's been amazing with the kids. I never thought I would be this happy. Everything is just so perfect."

"The kids!" Maggie exclaimed. "He's met your kids? You have to tell me all about it! But let's talk in the kitchen. I haven't eaten since breakfast and I'm starting to feel a little queasy."

In the kitchen, Morgan showed Maggie around, pointing out where the different food items were. In the pantry, they could hear an odd banging sound and a low moan, but they couldn't place the source. One minute it sounded as though it came from beneath them, and the next, it was as if it was coming from inside the wall.

"That's strange," Morgan remarked. "It sounds like a washing machine with bricks, but this house doesn't have a basement." Shrugging, she stepped out of the pantry to a very pale-faced Maggie. "What's the matter? You look like you've seen a ghost," she asked, allowing the pantry door to close behind her.

Maggie sat abruptly on a stool she had located. Eventually, her eyes refocused and she wondered aloud, "I don't know what that was. All of a sudden, I just had goose pimples and felt so dizzy. But I feel fine now." She appeared to be self-conscious for a moment, then chuckled to herself. "It must be the pregnancy," she concluded. "What should we eat? I'm famished!"

Morgan looked relieved as Maggie's coloring returned to normal. She placed a loaf of bread on the counter, asking, "Are you sure you feel okay, Mag? Maybe we should take you in and get you checked out."

"No, no, I'm fine; really," Maggie assured. "Besides, I'm not rushing to the hospital every time I feel…pregnant. That would be silly." She fixed Morgan with a confident stare that she hoped was suffused with the self-assurance she was striving to muster. "Now: what do you have to eat, or are you gonna make this pregnant girl starve?"

Morgan giggled and went to the fridge, rummaging through the crisper drawer until she found some lunchmeat and cheese. "Mayo or mustard?" she asked, as she placed them both on the counter. "Spinach!" Morgan exclaimed in response to her own question, returning to the vegetables she had just seen. After piling several veggies onto the island counter, she said, "Go see if the guys are hungry, why don't you, and I'll put my magic sub-making skills to work."

Maggie giggled back at her and walked to the door of John's office. "It's locked," she announced, puzzled over the unmoving knob.

Morgan frowned at the door, as if her expression alone could open it, and set the food items on the counter. "That's strange. In all the time I've been here, I don't think it's ever been locked." As if her verbalized statement was in tandem with her realization, she moved toward the hallway, and then to the door that entered the study from the hall. Finding it ajar, she stepped inside, followed closely by Maggie.

The two entered John's office and looked around. Neither of the men were there, leaving both women confused.

"I didn't hear the alarm beep; they couldn't have left the house. I wonder if they're upstairs."

As Morgan spoke those words, creaking could be heard from behind John's massive desk, followed by an unintelligible sound that could be best-described as a low grumbling, intermingled with wordless shouts.

When Seamus emerged from a hidden door next to John's overlarge chair, the cause of the strange noises became clear. Maggie's jaw dropped at the sight of her father as she worked to comprehend what she was seeing.

Seamus looked quite disheveled, covered in sweat and blood, and nearly every visible surface of his skin was battered and bruised. His hands had cuts around the palms that overlapped his bloodied, swollen knuckles.

When he saw the women staring at him in shocked awe, his forward motion stopped for a moment, but then he was bumped into from behind by Shannon, whose state of disarray was similar to Seamus's. Looking for the source of the obstruction, Shannon was mortified to realize that Maggie was in the room. He was visibly relieved when she sat down instead of running through the open door away from him. Noting her paleness, however, it was likely involuntary.

Shannon did not stand still for long, but instead went to Maggie, scooping her up before he sat on the couch with her. She could not make sense of what she was going on, but was thankful that Shannon was there, and her face automatically turned toward him, as she sought comfort. What she found, however, was the smell of blood, which caused a violent tremble to begin deep within her.

As he held her, she was shaking so intensely that he was forced to wrap both arms around her torso, and place one leg over her thighs. The weak, whimpering sounds that escaped her throat became louder as he stroked her hair.

"My God, you're covered in blood! Can't you see she's terrified? Take your shirt off!" Morgan shouted angrily, prompting him to look down at Maggie's face, which was up against his chest. Seeing the condition she was in, he moved her just enough so that he could remove his shirt, and then held her against his bare chest. She immediately settled against him and began to relax, as he violently threw the soiled shirt across the room.

"What the hell is going on here?" Morgan demanded, glaring at John. He had just emerged from the hidden door, wiping his bloodied hands on a dirty towel. She examined his disheveled and sweat-sodden appearance, stopping when she got to his hands.

The room was completely quiet except for Maggie's sniffling, and the soothing sounds that Shannon was breathing into her ear. When no explanation was offered, Morgan stomped past Seamus toward the secret door, only to be stopped by John grabbing her upper arm, effectively halting her movements.

She looked down at her bicep in John's iron grip, then back at his face. With a sneer, she spat, "If you ever want to hold me again, you will let go of me right now."

John had to sense that she wasn't bluffing, and Morgan could see it in his eyes. She thought he would unhand her, but instead he plead with his eyes and his words, "I will let you go, *a ghra mo chroi*, but I beg of you, please do not leave this house until you have listened to my explanation. Please!" He spoke the word "please" very quietly, but emphatically, as he released his grip on her.

She took a last wide-eyed look around that encompassed his desperate visage, as well as the two bloodied men and Maggie, and turned, cautiously descending the stairs that had been concealed by the hidden door. The stairwell was dimly lit, and she felt fear creeping up her spine. She attempted to slow her breathing and remain calm.

A few seconds later, Morgan came to an open room that reminded her of a medieval dungeon. Peering into the darkness, it took a moment to make out a still supine figure…a dismembered and maimed figure…disfigured so badly that it took all of her rational mind to recognize that it was a human body. Of its own volition, her mouth opened, and a scream worked its way up to her throat, only to be stopped by a hand being clamped over her gaping mouth.

Without the aid of conscious thought, her instinct took over, and she bit the hand, thrashing wildly while kicking and striking at anything that came near her. She struggled endlessly with the hand over her mouth until the adrenaline was finally exhausted from her body. When the powerful arms tentatively began to loosen their hold on her, she had no energy or strength left to fight her captor.

After an endless and fathomless period of time, Morgan realized that she was sitting and that the appendages of the unseen monster, as she had begun to think of her captor, were only loosely holding her. She began to devise a plan to escape its grasp. However, in devising her escape route, she must have tensed up, as the arms retightened their shackling grip on her.

After several moments, she gradually became aware of whispered words close to her ear. Comforted by them, she listened for an indeterminable amount of time, her face turning toward the voice. Eventually, she realized that it was John's, and that he was caressing her face and speaking softly to her. Suddenly, her reality fragmented when her eyes moved across the room, once again taking in the mutilated corpse while simultaneously taking in the sensations John was creating. She soon began to hyperventilate, as her vision tunneled.

John held Morgan closer when she began to panic again, cradling her into his body. He whispered words and songs to her until she calmed. Eventually, he began speaking to her.

"I hoped to keep this from you, my love, knowing it would be a horrible shock. How would this kind of carnage not be for a golden person such as yourself?" John asked her. Her breathing remained calm, but had changed so he knew that she was hearing him; that he was getting through to her.

"What I wished to explain to you before you came to see this horror, is that this bloody heap o' disgusting human filth is none other than the animal tha' hurt ye're dear friend upstairs." As he confessed, Morgan's body relaxed slightly into his and he became hopeful that she would believe him, and that he would not lose her.

Everything in John's world was riding on her acceptance of the justice that he and his countrymen had meted out for her friend. If she left him over the news, it was likely she would report him, and he would spend his life in prison and away from all he loved. For hours it seemed, they sat in the darkened basement, suspended in a state of purgatory, holding on to each other as if their lives depended on it.

Finally, as if her internal struggles had led her to a decision, the tension melted from her, and she took a deep breath. After turning in his lap to face him, she asked him while looking him directly in the eyes, "That mutilated, bloody, and beaten body is… the bastard doctor's? You three did that? You tortured him? For what he did to Maggie?"

John's arms were looped around her, resting on her hips when he answered her calmly, and with utter confidence, "Yes, Morgan. Yes to all of your questions, and I don't regret a single moment of it. And I would never take any part of it back, unless you were to leave me for it."

She seemed to be listening as he spoke his last words, her hands gripping his shoulders.

He pulled her closer and admitted, "I would still do the same, but would assure your absence from my home at present, so that you would never need be aware of such savage necessity or actions."

She took her time with his confession, and then answered the unasked question that preyed on his mind. "I will not leave you this day, my love, or any other, as long as you care for me and mine in such a heroic way."

She was silent for a moment, but he did not interject, sensing that was she would say more.

"I could never condemn you: a man of such honor, for ridding this world of one as evil as that wicked doctor." She grew quiet once more, but finally told him, "You are the opposite, my love. The way I see it is that you have done humanity a favor, doling out justice that would have otherwise been unlikely. The detectives said that he did something similar to this when he was in college and was able to get away with it because of his family's money and influence."

He waited patiently while she made her speech, but upon her finishing, he pulled her close and kissed her. When their affections slowed somewhat, she pulled back, looked at him with concern in her eyes and asked, "But John, I wonder…that is…what are you going to do with the body?"

He was unconcerned by the question; a question which most law-abiding citizens would be most worried over. His lips turned up into a smile that didn't quite reach his eyes, and he answered logically, "Dispose of it properly of course, *mo shearc*."

She smiled wryly at him, replying, "Of course."

Not wishing to dwell in the dungeon with the mutilated corpse any longer, John stood, carrying Morgan close to his chest as he did so in order to prevent her from seeing the body. He then ascended the stairs, her body cradled against his.

Being held in her lover's arms, Morgan was able to remain calm; that is until she remembered her best friend awaiting her return just above her.

Once they returned to the study, the scene was much different than before. Maggie was sitting on the couch with Shannon and her father on either side of her, tending to some of Seamus's more extensive injuries. When she saw the couple emerge from the hidden door, she exclaimed, "Morgan! Are you all right? I heard the strangest sounds while you were down there!"

Morgan nodded, then began to fret over how she was going to tell Maggie what had transpired in the dark room behind her. Finally, she decided that being blunt was the way Maggie always preferred difficult news, and announced, after ensuring that the study doors were closed, "You don't have to be worried about that bastard doctor anymore, Maggie. They took care of him for you."

Maggie smiled up at her happily, exclaiming, "I know! That's why they're so torn up. They hurt him while they were killing him."

Morgan blinked in confusion at her friend's reaction and wondered if her sanity had cracked; she looked entirely too happy to be discussing dismemberment and death, even if it was in regards to a worthless piece (or pieces, she amended sardonically in her mind) of human carcass like the one over which they were now standing.

Distractedly, while wrapping a bandage around her father's hand, Maggie told Morgan, "Killing him was the only way to make sure he didn't do it to someone else because believe me when I tell you this: perpetrators who are that violent have had lots of practice. So he has done things like this before. And he wouldn't have stopped." She pulled the Ace tight, and then gently patted his hand, gesturing that she was finished with her wound care. Shannon sported similar bandages on both of his hands.

With her work complete, Maggie looked again to Morgan and said, "Dismembering the body is the best way to get rid of it." She swallowed before continuing, stating with no apologies or remorse for the late Dr. David Schambaugh, "They just started it while he was still alive." She held Morgan's eye contact as she said this, letting her know without words, that she felt that the consequences had been fair for the horrible crimes he had committed.

Morgan nodded in agreement before collapsing onto John's lap, where he had seated himself in the chair behind his desk.

The room was quiet for some time until Shannon addressed Morgan, "I'd already gotten him, ye see, when me dear Maggie was at the hospital still."

Morgan was startled at the admission but asked, "You mean…wait…how long have you had him?"

Shannon watched Morgan as the comprehension dawned in her eyes, and explained, "Aye. I snatched 'im up jus' after 'e dropped 'er like a pile o' rags on 'er door step. 'e wasna so good at fightin' agains' one his own size, so it wasna a problem fer me to grab 'im."

Shannon had the attention of both women, but the other men in the room avoided looking at him, already aware of what he would confess.

"I didna ken wha' to do with 'im at first, so I tossed 'im in me trunk after knockin' 'im out good, and while I was sittin' by his place, I saw Seamus an' the garda there, I ken I was on the right path, so I jus' held onto the wee bastard for a bit."

Maggie had repositioned herself so that her head was against Shannon's shoulder and his hand was in her lap, where she squeezed it in encouragement from time to time. His other hand stroked her hair absentmindedly.

"When did you bring him here?" Morgan asked curiously, without the slightest hint of condemnation in her voice. John answered, while his grip on her tightened considerably.

"It was the morning she was taken to the hospital; it had to have been just after he did all of that to her. That's when Shannon called me and told me what he had seen, and what he had with him." He looked Morgan in the eye as he continued. "Of course, I told him to bring the animal here, and here is where he has stayed since...until..." John paused.

"...until we took out of 'im what he did to my daughter. An' then we didna let him die until she came here so tha' he could look at her face as he went from this world to the next, and know tha' he didna kill her beauty or her spirit with his evil acts." Seamus interrupted John with his impassioned speech.

Maggie smiled gratefully at her father and hugged him tightly, nestling herself in between the two men.

Suddenly, the front door to the house opened, spurning them all into action.

"Hello? Is anyone home?" came Jasmine's voice, echoing off of the walls in the hallway.

John was the first to the door and motioned her into the office. "We're back here, wife," he called to her.

Just then, Jasmine walked into the office with Patrick following closely behind her. When the two entered the room, they appeared taken aback by everyone present. However their excitement was palpable.

Shannon looked at Patrick and urged, "Ye've good news to tell us old friend? Be out wit' it then. We could use some cheerin'."

Patrick's hands ascended Jasmine's back, and then began to massage her shoulders and neck. "Go on then, love," he encouraged her, smiling.

A half breath after the words left his mouth, she ecstatically exclaimed, "I'm pregnant! Isn't that great news?!"

The room was silent for a moment, until John irritably scolded her. "How can you think this such a cause for celebration, Jasmine? Do you even know whose it is? It could be a bastard for all we know."

Patrick defensively stepped out from behind Jasmine as soon as the words had left his brother's mouth, and socked him in the orifice that had just made the statement. "Donut ye dare ter talk te her tha' way." His deep voice boomed within the confines of the room.

John was stunned, but quickly gave his brother a blow of his own, in the nose, so that he began bleeding.

Morgan could see where the exchange was going, although she couldn't say that she blamed Patrick for being angry; in fact she agreed that John deserved to be manhandled for such a rude statement. Stepping around the skirmish, she put her arm around Jasmine's shoulder, inviting her, along with Maggie, into the kitchen. "I could really use some tea right now. Why don't you two join me?"

Maggie took one last look at the two brothers rolling around on the floor, attempting to wallop each other, and stood up and accompanied her friend out of the study, followed by Shannon. Seamus remained seated, enjoying his front-row entertainment.

In the kitchen, Morgan finished assembling the sandwiches she had started earlier, and the group conversed about nothing in particular, other than awkward small talk and occasional requests for the passing of condiments or napkins.

When the meal was finished, and through intermittent thumps and groans from the office, both Morgan and Jasmine had become quite anxious and irascible. Finally, Morgan turned to Jasmine, suggesting, "Let's go break up this ridiculous squabbling before one of our boys gets hurt."

Jasmine agreed and followed her, leaving Shannon and Maggie alone. He didn't fail to notice, and invited her to accompany him to their bedroom.

When Morgan and Jasmine stepped into John's study, the room was in such disarray that the only piece of furniture that was still upright were those that were likely too heavy to be casually lifted. In the center of the wreckage, John, Patrick, and Seamus sat on the floor, laughing raucously, and passing a bottle of scotch between themselves. Irritably, Morgan noted that where they were seated was the only clear space large enough to contain all three of the large male bodies.

"Are we done?" Morgan demanded, glaring at the men.

In unison, their glasses raised at the ladies in mock toast. "Yes, we are!" they all exclaimed, at different intervals and on top of each other, which elicited another roar of hearty guffaws.

As the room quieted down, John stood and walked toward the two women. He looked, first at Jasmine, and then at Morgan, holding her gaze.

After several seconds of the two watching each other, John turned to Jasmine, took her hand in his, and brought it to his lips and kissed it. "Please forgive me, my wife, and the beloved of my brother…and the lovely mother of our children." At this, he bowed to her, and then kneeled on one knee, still clasping her hand. Looking up at her, he asked sincerely, "Can you ever find it in your gracious heart to forgive me?"

Jasmine seemed unsure of how to take him behaving in such a submissive manner, and looked first to Morgan, before her eyes settled on Patrick, in an attempt to find some assistance.

Seeing her insecurity at his most un-John-like, non-dominant behavior, John decided to help and relieve her discomfort. "You don't have to forgive me right now, lovely lady of my kin. I only ask that you continue to be as gracious a mother to all of our children as you have been for all of your motherhood." With this, he stood while retaining her hand, placed one last kiss over her knuckles, and released her.

When John moved toward Morgan, Patrick went to Jasmine's side, and asked, "Can I take ye home across the street, *a ghra mo chroi*? All of this drink ha' made me hungry for ye're love."

Jasmine smiled at him, and then gingerly touched the blossoming bruise that lay just beneath his eye. "I would like nothing more, my love," she answered before the two made their way through the front door, leaving behind John, Morgan, and Seamus.

That did not last for long, however, because John turned to his lover, kissing her deeply, forgetting that they were not alone. When his passion drove him to grope the front of her shirt, she stopped him, suggesting urgently, "Let's go upstairs now." The two set off, taking the stairs in doubles so that they could get to the master suite and gain access to each other.

Their night was spent in sheer ecstasy.

A Glimpse Down the Road

Maggie was awakened by the bright summer sun warming her face, and Shannon's hand settling on her abdomen, pulling her into his burgeoning erection. She initially thought to place her hand around his shaft, and then after vigorously stroking him, take him into her mouth. But after careful consideration, she thought better of it, pulling away from his smothering grip while pushing on his shoulder until he was lying on his back.

Thankful that they had each settled into the habit of sleeping nude, she lifted herself, encompassing her protruding abdomen, stretched tight over their growing child. She straddled him, enjoying the feel, as his invasion ignorantly but passionately pushed aside the silken creases of her feminine channel.

A sensuous moan escaped his lips, and she rocked her hips back and forth, riding him. After several moments of her slow and sensuous glide, his hands found their way to her hips, feeling the subtly protruding bones, and then ascended past them and her waist, to rest, cupping the soft weight of her breasts.

As his fingertips swirled over her hardening nipples, his eyes opened just enough so that he looked up at her through slits in his eyelids. Abruptly, his palms returned to her hips, grasping her firmly to prevent her from moving. He then demanded, "What in bloody hell do ye think ye're doing? Ye'll hurt the babe. You know we canna do this, now move off," while gently pushing at her.

Usually, when he would push her away from him, she would willingly accept it. Her high risk pregnancy doctor had told them that intercourse- or anything in the vagina, for that matter- was off-limits and potentially dangerous to the fragile life that she carried within her womb. However, today was different. She had been to see her maternal-fetal medicine physician the previous day and had been cleared for intercourse. The subchorionic hematoma that was likely the result of the violence she had sustained at the hands of her abuser, and that had caused her to have intermittent bleeding and cramping throughout the earlier parts of the pregnancy, had resolved itself.

Grasping his wrists in her hands, she pulled them away from her and pushed them into the mattress. While looking him in the eye, she hovered over him and stated assertively, "No. I will not move off, Mr. Kelly. I will have what is mine."

Shannon had been watching her, deliberating their situation through half-lidded eyes, but as Maggie had become more and more forceful, his eyes opened wide and he studied her face. His expressions belied the emotions swirling beneath the surface as his hands grasped the hips that hovered over his more firmly this time.

"Aye. Yours I am, me love, but I willna risk me lil' one jus' fer me balls ter have a taste of ye're box." His hand had continued their grasp on her hips, but as he presented his rationale, they loosened, sure she would relent, once he made his perspective known.

Unfortunately for Shannon, that was not the case. Maggie pulled his hands into hers, thus pulling them away from where they had settled, restraining her. After strategically placing them at her breasts to grope and fondle, and after they had time to become content with the placement there, she resumed her slow rhythmic glide, riding him, while his fingers swirled over her nipples.

When he tensed, she held his hands to the perch they had found, stating, "No, you don't. You will not stop." Contrary to her command, his hips stopped gyrating and his thrusts into her subsided.

"Wha' in bloody hell do ye think ye're doin'?" he asked her, staring daggers at her. She remained calm, answering, "I'm making love to you, and Dr. Smith said it was okay. I'm no longer at risk."

He studied her for a moment. It was easy to do, as she was perched over him with her heavy breasts swaying, enticing him. Though he wanted nothing more than to bury his cock deep inside of her where it belonged, it would not be worth threatening the life of the wee babby she carried, and he contemplated her offer with a guarded sense of joy and desire.

When Shannon could sense no feminine wiles playing out, and considered Maggie's anguish each time she thought the pregnancy at risk, he decided that she was not being like his wife and using her natural assets as a means to manipulate and get what she wanted. Unable to keep hold of the tight reins in which he had leashed his desire for her through sheer stubborn willpower alone, he groped her shoulders and rolled her over, mounting her.

He looked into her face, judging her response as he aggressively told her, "I canna stop once I start. I have wanted ye so much fer so long." After pausing to let it sink in, he pleaded with her, "Please, *mo fiorghra*, tell me now if it isna so. Can I have ye without worryin' about the babe?"

Maggie smiled her bright and serene smile, assuring him, "Yes, Shannon. I am yours. Take me. It will not hurt our baby."

With this permission, Shannon unleashed the control he had on himself and then captured her mouth, suckling her bottom lip in between his. He kissed her passionately as he pushed into her, slowly at first.

As the contact between their mouths intensified, so did his passion, and he was finding that he could no longer maintain his control. He began driving deeper and deeper into her, tentatively at first, testing the environment of her risky pregnancy.

When her reaction met his with moan after moan and thrust after thrust, he could hold back no longer, and began pounding into her. Intermittently, he brought his mouth to her face and tasted her lips while their tango slowed. But each time, the short respite was renewed by a dynamic passion that they shared. They had each been starved for the touch of the other for so long; an absence that had them moving vigorously against each other in an effort to make up for the many months they had been forbidden from enjoying that which they so desperately needed from the other. Their energy was spent heatedly in an effort to make up for that lost time.

Shannon was quickly losing all control and didn't think he could refrain from climaxing. He looked Maggie in the eye for a moment, and then watched the junction where their body met, searching for signs that all was not well, looking for hemorrhage. When he received nothing but unbridled pleasure with the delicious pressure becoming too much for him, his hips moved frantically in an effort to gain the all-encompassing release that he knew she wanted as well.

"Tell me ye want it!" he commanded, causing her to track him through glazed eyes.

"Please, Shannon! I want you! Please! Give it to me!" He pistoned into her roughly, eliciting a throaty moan and a last thrust of hips meeting hips, unable to hold back any longer. Giving in to the sweet release that he had so desperately sought, he buried himself in her one last time, and then collapsed on top of her.

The two worked to catch their breath and then settled in together, breathing in the scent of sex, mingled with the musky odor of sweaty skin and the desperate lust of being in close quarters with a lover who was just out of reach.

After kissing passionately, they settled into the mattress together and slept for a bit, blissfully happy, and satisfied that the path that lay before them would be a good one.

End of Book 3